Incredible Tales
of the
SEA

D1373976

Incredible Tales
of the
SEA

Twelve Classic Sailing Stories

EDITED BY

TOM McCARTHY

THE LYONS PRESS
GUILFORD, CONNECTICUT
AN IMPRINT OF THE GLOBE PEQUOT PRESS

The Lyons Press is an imprint of The Globe Pequot Press.

10   9   8   7   6   5   4   3   2   1

Printed in the United States of America

ISBN 1-59228-811-1

Library of Congress Cataloging-in-Publication Data
is available on file.

To Newton:
A True Sea Dog

Contents

CONTENTS

Introduction

Why are sea stories so enduringly popular? Why is it tales of the sea, more than perhaps any other genre, are so appealing to so many readers? There is the adventure, of course, and the vicarious thrill of taking on the Horn or battling attacking pirates or surviving great privation from the comfort of one's dry and warm living room. Reading the stories in this volume is much safer than actually participating in similar adventures. But that's the magic of it: pick up a book and transport yourself to William Bligh's boat or Robinson Crusoe's island. Put the book down and go pick the kids up at soccer practice. Instant adventure with no hassles. Return trips at no extra charge. And there are no special requirements to join.

The stories offered here, I hope, are by turns, entertaining, dramatic, exciting, and eminently readable. All have withstood the test of time, and all have been enjoyed by generations of readers. Many are excerpted from larger works, and I can only encourage you to seek out the originals. At the risk of waxing purple, writers have long turned to the sea for inspiration and backdrop. *Incredible Tales of the Sea* is but a small taste, but I hope a filling one.

Robert Louis Stevenson wrote *Treasure Island*, from which "The Treasure Hunt" is excerpted, for his stepson in 1818 and is reported to have said "If this don't fetch the kids, they have gone rotten since my day." Kids aside, *Treasure Island* is an enduring classic that works as well for adults. Who doesn't love a tale of pirates and treasure and duplicity?

Daniel Defoe wrote his novel *Robinson Crusoe*, from which "A Perilous Voyage" is taken, in 1719. DeFoe is believed to have based his novel on the true story of the shipwreck of Scotsman Alexander Selkirk.

The prolific Victor Hugo is better known for the landbound *Notre Dame de Paris* and *Les Miserables*, but on occasion he took to the sea. "An Imprisoned Thunderstorm" is taken from his admittedly obscure novel *Ninety-Three*.

William Bligh's masterful and heroic voyage with eighteen of his sailors in a twenty-three-foot open launch is considered one of the greatest examples of seamanship on record. Cast out from the *Bounty*, he had a sextant and a pocketwatch but no charts. He successfully navigated 3,618 nautical miles in forty-one days. His understated account of part of that voyage can be found in "Passage Toward New Holland."

Homer's classic, *The Odyssey*, a short but exciting section of which you'll find in "The Test," recounts the ten-year journey of Odysseus (here using the Latin name Ulysses) on his way home to Ithaca from Troy.

Herman Melville, perhaps the greatest writer of his time, appears twice in this volume, the only author so chosen. And why not? During his lifetime his early novels were popular, but he later suffered from a dwindling audience. He's now regarded as one of the most important figures in American literature. "A Draft in a Man-of-War" is excerpted from *White-Jacket*, "A Fatal Mistake" from *Billy Budd*.

While justifiably known for his prodigious library of science fiction, the sea and ships had long held sway for Jules Verne. As a young man he ran off to be a cabin boy but was caught and returned to his parents. After acquiring vast wealth through the sale of his books, he bought a yacht and sailed to many European ports. "An Unknown Species of Whale" is excerpted from *20,000 Leagues Under the Sea*.

The harsh and unforgiving waters off the coast of Iceland are some of the richest fishing areas in the world. "When I Was on the Frigate" is the work of Icelander Jón Trausti (a pen name of Gudmundor Magnusson), a writer who once worked as a fisherman.

Richard Hakluyt was a sixteenth-century geographer and clergyman who edited and translated many volumes of first-hand narratives of seagoing adventurers. "The Rescue" shows how little some things have changed as it recounts John Fox's rescue of Christians in 1577 from the group of angry Muslims who held them captive at Alexandria.

No collection of sea stories is complete without a tale of shipwreck. Charles Dickens heads seaward for the "Wreck of the Golden Mary."

I hope readers will find this collection compelling and entertaining. The great pleasure of reading though an enormous volume of terrific stories made the entire project effortless.

Tom McCarthy
Chester, Connecticut
October 2005

Incredible Tales
of the
SEA

The Treasure Hunt

[ROBERT LOUIS STEVENSON]

Partly from the damping influence of this alarm, partly to rest Silver and the sick folk, the whole party sat down as soon as they had gained the brow of the ascent.

The plateau being somewhat tilted towards the west, this spot on which we had paused commanded a wide prospect on either hand. Before us, over the tree-tops, we beheld the Cape of the Woods fringed with surf; behind, we not only looked down upon the anchorage and Skeleton Island, but saw—clear across the spit and the eastern lowlands—a great field of open sea upon the east. Sheer above us rose the Spy-glass, here dotted with single pines, there black with precipices. There was no sound but that of the distant breakers, mounting from all round, and the chirp of countless insects in the brush. Not a man, not a sail, upon the sea; the very largeness of the view increased the sense of solitude.

Silver, as he sat, took certain bearings with his compass.

"There are three 'tall trees'," said he, "about in the right line from Skeleton Island. 'Spy-glass shoulder,' I take it, means that lower p'int there. It's child's play to find the stuff now. I've half a mind to dine first."

"I don't feel sharp," growled Morgan. "Thinkin' o' Flint—I think it were—as done me."

"Ah, well, my son, you praise your stars he's dead," said Silver.

"He were an ugly devil," cried a third pirate with a shudder; "that blue in the face too!"

"That was how the rum took him," added Merry. "Blue! Well, I reckon he was blue. That's a true word."

Ever since they had found the skeleton and got upon this train of thought, they had spoken lower and lower, and they had almost got to whispering by now, so that the sound of their talk hardly interrupted the silence of the wood. All of a sudden, out of the middle of the trees in front of us, a thin, high, trembling voice struck up the well-known air and words:

"Fifteen men on the dead man's chest—
Yo-ho-ho, and a bottle of rum!"

I never have seen men more dreadfully affected than the pirates. The colour went from their six faces like enchantment; some leaped to their feet, some clawed hold of others; Morgan grovelled on the ground.

"It's Flint, by ——!" cried Merry.

The song had stopped as suddenly as it began—broken off, you would have said, in the middle of a note, as though someone had laid his hand upon the singer's mouth. Coming through the clear, sunny atmosphere among the green tree-tops, I thought it had sounded airily and sweetly; and the effect on my companions was the stranger.

"Come," said Silver, struggling with his ashen lips to get the word out; "this won't do. Stand by to go about. This is a rum start, and I can't name the voice, but it's someone skylarking—someone that's flesh and blood, and you may lay to that."

His courage had come back as he spoke, and some of the colour to his face along with it. Already the others had begun to lend an ear to this encouragement and were coming a little to themselves, when the same voice broke out again—not this time singing, but in a faint distant hail that echoed yet fainter among the clefts of the Spy-glass.

"Darby M'Graw," it wailed—for that is the word that best describes the sound—"Darby M'Graw! Darby M'Graw!" again and again and again; and then rising a little higher, and with an oath that I leave out: "Fetch aft the rum, Darby!"

The buccaneers remained rooted to the ground, their eyes starting from their heads. Long after the voice had died away they still stared in silence, dreadfully, before them.

"That fixes it!" gasped one. "Let's go."

"They was his last words," moaned Morgan, "his last words above board."

Dick had his Bible out and was praying volubly. He had been well brought up, had Dick, before he came to sea and fell among bad companions.

Still Silver was unconquered. I could hear his teeth rattle in his head, but he had not yet surrendered.

"Nobody in this here island ever heard of Darby," he muttered; "not one but us that's here." And then, making a great effort: "Shipmates," he cried, "I'm here to get that stuff, and I'll not be beat by man or devil. I never was feared of Flint in his life, and, by the powers, I'll face him dead. There's seven hundred thousand pound not a quarter of a mile from here. When did ever a gentleman o' fortune show his stern to that much dollars for a boozy old seaman with a blue mug—and him dead too?"

But there was no sign of reawakening courage in his followers, rather, indeed, of growing terror at the irreverence of his words.

"Belay there, John!" said Merry. "Don't you cross a sperrit."

And the rest were all too terrified to reply. They would have run away severally had they dared; but fear kept them together, and kept them close by John, as if his daring helped them. He, on his part, had pretty well fought his weakness down.

"Sperrit? Well, maybe," he said. "But there's one thing not clear to me. There was an echo. Now, no man ever seen a sperrit with a shadow; well then, what's he doing with an echo to him, I should like to know? That ain't in natur', surely?"

This argument seemed weak enough to me. But you can never tell what will affect the superstitious, and to my wonder, George Merry was greatly relieved.

"Well, that's so," he said. "You've a head upon your shoulders, John, and no mistake. 'Bout ship, mates! This here crew is on a wrong tack, I do believe. And come to think on it, it was like Flint's voice, I grant you, but not just so clear-away like it, after all. It was liker somebody else's voice now—it was liker—"

"By the powers, Ben Gunn!" roared Silver.

"Aye, and so it were," cried Morgan, springing on his knees. "Ben Gunn it were!"

"It don't make much odds, do it, now?" asked Dick. "Ben Gunn's not here in the body any more'n Flint."

But the older hands greeted this remark with scorn.

"Why, nobody minds Ben Gunn," cried Merry; "dead or alive, nobody minds him."

It was extraordinary how their spirits had returned and how the natural colour had revived in their faces. Soon they were chatting together, with intervals of listening; and not long after, hearing no further sound, they shouldered the tools and set forth again, Merry walking first with Silver's compass to keep them on the right line with Skeleton Island. He had said the truth: dead or alive, nobody minded Ben Gunn.

Dick alone still held his Bible, and looked around him as he went, with fearful glances; but he found no sympathy, and Silver even joked him on his precautions.

"I told you," said he—"I told you you had sp'iled your Bible. If it ain't no good to swear by, what do you suppose a sperrit would give for it? Not that!" and he snapped his big fingers, halting a moment on his crutch.

But Dick was not to be comforted; indeed, it was soon plain to me that the lad was falling sick; hastened by heat, exhaustion, and the shock of his alarm, the fever, predicted by Dr. Livesey, was evidently growing swiftly higher.

It was fine open walking here, upon the summit; our way lay a little downhill, for, as I have said, the plateau tilted towards the west. The pines, great and small, grew wide apart; and even between the clumps of nutmeg and azalea, wide open spaces baked in the hot sunshine. Striking, as we did, pretty near north-west across the island, we drew, on the one hand, ever nearer under the shoulders of the Spy-glass, and on the other, looked ever wider over that western bay where I had once tossed and trembled in the oracle.

The first of the tall trees was reached, and by the bearings proved the wrong one. So with the second. The third rose nearly two hundred feet into the air above a clump of underwood—a giant of a veg-etable, with a red column as big as a cottage, and a wide shadow around in which a company could have manoeuvred. It was conspicuous far to sea both on the east and west and might have been entered as a sailing mark upon the chart.

But it was not its size that now impressed my companions; it was the knowledge that seven hun-dred thousand pounds in gold lay somewhere buried below its spreading shadow. The thought of the money, as they drew nearer, swallowed up their pre-vious terrors. Their eyes burned in their heads; their feet grew speedier and lighter; their whole soul was found up in that fortune, that whole lifetime of ex-travagance and pleasure, that lay waiting there for each of them.

Silver hobbled, grunting, on his crutch; his nostrils stood out and quivered; he cursed like a madman when the flies settled on his hot and shiny counte-nance; he plucked furiously at the line that held me to him and from time to time turned his eyes upon me with a deadly look. Certainly he took no pains to hide his thoughts, and certainly I read them like print. In the immediate nearness of the gold, all else had been forgotten: his promise and the doctor's warning were both things of the past, and I could not doubt that he hoped to seize upon the treasure, find and board the *Hispaniola* under cover of night, cut every honest throat about that island, and sail away as he had at first intended, laden with crimes and riches.

Shaken as I was with these alarms, it was hard for me to keep up with the rapid pace of the treasure-hunters. Now and again I stumbled, and it was then that Silver plucked so roughly at the rope and launched at me his murderous glances. Dick, who had dropped behind us and now brought up the rear, was babbling to himself both prayers and curses as his fever kept rising. This also added to my wretchedness, and to crown all, I was haunted by the thought of the tragedy that had once been acted on that plateau, when that ungodly buccaneer with the blue face—he who died at Savannah, singing and shouting for drink—had there, with his own hand, cut down his six accomplices. This grove that was now so peaceful must then have rung with cries, I thought; and even with the thought I could believe I heard it ringing still.

We were now at the margin of the thicket. "Huzza, mates, all together!" shouted Merry; and the foremost broke into a run.

And suddenly, not ten yards further, we beheld them stop. A low cry arose. Silver doubled his pace, digging away with the foot of his crutch like one possessed; and next moment he and I had come also to a dead halt.

Before us was a great excavation, not very recent, for the sides had fallen in and grass had sprouted on the bottom. In this were the shaft of a pick broken in two and the boards of several packing-cases strewn around. On one of these boards I saw, branded with a hot iron, the name *Walrus*—the name of Flint's ship.

All was clear to probation. The cache had been found and rifled; the seven hundred thousand pounds were gone!

There never was such an overturn in this world. Each of these six men was as though he had been struck. But with Silver the blow passed almost instantly. Every thought of his soul had been set full-stretch, like a racer, on that money; well, he was brought up, in a single second, dead; and he kept his head, found his temper, and changed his plan before the others had had time to realize the disappointment.

"Jim," he whispered, "take that, and stand by for trouble."

And he passed me a double-barrelled pistol.

At the same time, he began quietly moving northward, and in a few steps had put the hollow between us two and the other five. Then he looked at me and nodded, as much as to say, "Here is a narrow corner," as, indeed, I thought it was. His looks were not quite friendly, and I was so revolted at these constant changes that I could not forbear whispering, "So you've changed sides again."

There was no time left for him to answer in. The buccaneers, with oaths and cries, began to leap, one after another, into the pit and to dig with their fingers, throwing the boards aside as they did so. Morgan found a piece of gold. He held it up with a perfect spout of oaths. It was a two-guinea piece, and it went from hand to hand among them for a quarter of a minute.

"Two guineas!" roared Merry, shaking it at Silver. "That's your seven hundred thousand pounds, is it? You're the man for bargains, ain't you? You're him that never bungled nothing, you wooden-headed lubber!"

"Dig away, boys," said Silver with the coolest insolence; "you'll find some pig-nuts and I shouldn't wonder."

"Pig-nuts!" repeated Merry, in a scream. "Mates, do you hear that? I tell you now, that man there knew it all along. Look in the face of him and you'll see it wrote there."

"Ah, Merry," remarked Silver, "standing for cap'n again? You're a pushing lad, to be sure."

But this time everyone was entirely in Merry's favour. They began to scramble out of the excavation, darting furious glances behind them. One thing I observed, which looked well for us: they all got out upon the opposite side from Silver.

Well, there we stood, two on one side, five on the other, the pit between us, and nobody screwed up high enough to offer the first blow. Silver never moved; he watched them, very upright on his crutch, and looked as cool as ever I saw him. He was brave, and no mistake.

At last Merry seemed to think a speech might help matters.

"Mates," says he, "there's two of them alone there; one's the old cripple that brought us all here and blundered us down to this; the other's that cub that I mean to have the heart of. Now, mates—"

He was raising his arm and his voice, and plainly meant to lead a charge. But just then—crack! crack! crack!—three musket-shots flashed out of the thicket. Merry tumbled head foremost into the excavation; the man with the bandage spun round like a teetotum and fell all his length upon his side, where he lay dead, but still twitching; and the other three turned and ran for it with all their might.

Before you could wink, Long John had fired two barrels of a pistol into the struggling Merry, and as the man rolled up his eyes at him in the last agony, "George," said he, "I reckon I settled you."

At the same moment, the doctor, Gray, and Ben Gunn joined us, with smoking muskets, from among the nutmeg-trees.

"Forward!" cried the doctor. "Double quick, my lads. We must head 'em off the boats."

And we set off at a great pace, sometimes plunging through the bushes to the chest.

I tell you, but Silver was anxious to keep up with us. The work that man went through, leaping on his crutch till the muscles of his chest were fit to burst, was work no sound man ever equalled; and so thinks the doctor. As it was, he was already thirty yards behind us and on the verge of strangling when we reached the brow of the slope.

"Doctor," he hailed, "see there! No hurry!"

Sure enough there was no hurry. In a more open part of the plateau, we could see the three survivors still running in the same direction as they had started, right for Mizzen-mast Hill. We were already between them and the boats; and so we four sat down to breathe, while Long John, mopping his face, came slowly up with us.

"Thank ye kindly, doctor," says he. "You came in about the nick, I guess, for me and Hawkins. And so it's you, Ben Gunn!" he added. "Well, you're a nice one, to be sure."

"I'm Ben Gunn, I am," replied the maroon, wriggling like an eel in his embarrassment. "And," he added, after a long pause, "how do, Mr. Silver? Pretty well, I thank ye, says you."

"Ben, Ben," murmured Silver, "to think as you've done me!"

The doctor sent back Gray for one of the pickaxes deserted, in their flight, by the mutineers, and then as we proceeded leisurely downhill to where the boats were lying, related in a few words what had taken place. It was a story that profoundly interested Silver; and Ben Gunn, the half-idiot maroon, was the hero from beginning to end.

Ben, in his long, lonely wanderings about the island, had found the skeleton—it was he that had rifled it; he had found the treasure; he had dug it up (it was the haft of his pick-axe that lay broken in the excavation); he had carried it on his back, in many weary journeys, from the foot of the tall pine to a cave he had on the two-pointed hill at the north-east angle of the island, and there it had lain stored in safety since two months before the arrival of the *Hispaniola*.

When the doctor had wormed this secret from him on the afternoon of the attack, and when next morning he saw the anchorage deserted, he had gone to Silver, given him the chart, which was now useless—given him the stores, for Ben Gunn's cave was well supplied with goats' meat salted by himself—given anything and everything to get a chance of moving in safety from the stockade to the two-pointed hill, there to be clear of malaria and keep a guard upon the money.

"As for you, Jim," he said, "it went against my heart, but I did what I thought best for those who had stood by their duty; and if you were not one of these, whose fault was it?"

That morning, finding that I was to be involved in the horrid disappointment he had prepared for the mutineers, he had run all the way to the cave, and leaving the squire to guard the captain, had taken Gray and the maroon and started, making the diagonal across the island to be at hand beside the pine. Soon, however, he saw that our party had the start of him; and Ben Gunn, being fleet of foot, had been dispatched in front to do his best alone. Then it had occurred to him to work upon the superstitions of his former shipmates, and he was so far successful that Gray and the doctor had come up and were already ambushed before the arrival of the treasure-hunters.

"Ah," said Silver, "it were fortunate for me that I had Hawkins here. You would have let old John be cut to bits, and never given it a thought, doctor."

"Not a thought," replied Dr. Livesey cheerily.

And by this time we had reached the gigs. The doctor, with the pick-axe, demolished one of them, and then we all got aboard the other and set out to go round by sea for North Inlet.

This was a run of eight or nine miles. Silver, though he was almost killed already with fatigue, was set to an oar, like the rest of us, and we were soon skimming swiftly over a smooth sea. Soon we passed out of the straits and doubled the south-east corner of the island, round which, four days ago, we had towed the *Hispaniola*.

As we passed the two-pointed hill, we could see the black mouth of Ben Gunn's cave and a figure standing by it, leaning on a musket. It was the squire, and we waved a handkerchief and gave him three cheers, in which the voice of Silver joined as heartily as any.

Three miles farther, just inside the mouth of North Inlet, what should we meet but the *Hispaniola*, cruising by herself? The last flood had lifted her, and had there been much wind or a strong tide current, as in the southern anchorage, we should never have found her more, or found her stranded beyond help. As it was, there was little amiss beyond the wreck of the main-sail. Another anchor was got ready and dropped in a fathom and a half of water. We all pulled round again to Rum Cove, the nearest point for Ben Gunn's treasure-house; and then Gray, single-handed, returned with the gig to the *Hispaniola*, where he was to pass the night on guard.

A gentle slope ran up from the beach to the entrance of the cave. At the top, the squire met us. To me he was cordial and kind, saying nothing of my escapade either in the way of blame or praise. At Silver's polite salute he somewhat flushed.

"John Silver," he said, "you're a prodigious villain and imposter—a monstrous imposter, sir. I am told I am not to prosecute you. Well, then, I will not. But the dead men, sir, hang about your neck like mill-stones."

"Thank you kindly, sir," replied Long John, again saluting.

"I dare you to thank me!" cried the squire. "It is a gross dereliction of my duty. Stand back."

And thereupon we all entered the cave. It was a large, airy place, with a little spring and a pool of clear water, overhung with ferns. The floor was sand. Before a big fire lay Captain Smollett; and in a far corner, only duskily flickered over by the blaze, I beheld great heaps of coin and quadrilaterals built of bars of gold. That was Flint's treasure that we had come so far to seek and that had cost already the lives of seventeen men from the *Hispaniola*. How many it had cost in the amassing, what blood and sorrow, what good ships scuttled on the deep, what brave men walking the plank blindfold, what shot of cannon, what shame and lies and cruelty, perhaps no man alive could tell. Yet there were still three upon that island—Silver, and old Morgan, and Ben Gunn—who had each taken his share in these crimes, as each had hoped in vain to share in the reward.

"Come in, Jim," said the captain. "You're a good boy in your line, Jim, but I don't think you and me'll go to sea again. You're too much of the born favourite for me. Is that you, John Silver? What brings you here, man?"

"Come back to my dooty, sir," returned Silver.

"Ah!" said the captain, and that was all he said.

What a supper I had of it that night, with all my friends around me; and what a meal it was, with Ben Gunn's salted goat and some delicacies and a bottle of old wine from the *Hispaniola*. Never, I am sure, were people gayer or happier. And there was Silver, sitting back almost out of the firelight, but eating heartily, prompt to spring forward when anything was wanted, even joining quietly in our laughter—the same bland, polite, obsequious seaman of the voyage out.

The next morning we fell early to work, for the transportation of this great mass of gold near a mile by land to the beach, and thence three miles by boat to the *Hispaniola*, was a considerable task for so small a number of workmen. The three fellows still abroad upon the island did not greatly trouble us; a single sentry on the shoulder of the hill was sufficient to ensure us against any sudden onslaught, and we thought, besides, they had had more than enough of fighting.

Therefore the work was pushed on briskly. Gray and Ben Gunn came and went with the boat, while the rest during their absences piled treasure on the beach. Two of the bars, slung in a rope's end, made a good load for a grown man—one that he was glad to walk slowly with. For my part, as I was not much use at carrying, I was kept busy all day in the cave packing the minted money into bread-bags.

It was a strange collection, like Billy Bones's hoard for the diversity of coinage, but so much larger and so much more varied that I think I never had more pleasure than in sorting them. English, French, Spanish, Portuguese, Georges, and Louises, doubloons and double guineas and moidores and sequins, the pictures of all the kings of Europe for the last hundred years, strange Oriental pieces stamped with what looked like wisps of string or bits of spider's web, round pieces and square pieces, and pieces bored through the middle, as if to wear them round your neck—nearly every variety of money in the world must, I think, have found a place in that collection; and for number, I am sure they were like autumn leaves, so that my back ached with stooping and my fingers with sorting them out.

Day after day this work went on; by every evening a fortune had been stowed aboard, but there was another fortune waiting for the morrow; and all this time we heard nothing of the three surviving mutineers.

At last—I think it was on the third night—the doctor and I were strolling on the shoulder of the hill where it overlooks the lowlands of the isle, when, from out of the thick darkness below, the wind brought us a noise between shrieking and singing. It was only a snatch that reached our ears, followed by the former silence.

"Heaven forgive them," said the doctor; "'tis the mutineers!"

"All drunk, sir," struck in the voice of Silver from behind us.

Silver, I should say, was allowed his entire liberty, and in spite of daily rebuffs, seemed to regard himself once more as quite a privileged and friendly dependent. Indeed, it was remarkable how well he bore these slights and with what unwearying politeness he kept on trying to ingratiate himself with all. Yet, I think, none treated him better than a dog, unless it was Ben Gunn, who was still terribly afraid of his old quartermaster, or myself, who had really something to thank him for; although for that matter, I suppose, I had reason to think even worse of him than anybody else, for I had seen him meditating a fresh treachery upon the plateau. Accordingly, it was pretty gruffly that the doctor answered him.

"Drunk or raving," said he.

"Right you were, sir," replied Silver; "and precious little odds which, to you and me."

"I suppose you would hardly ask me to call you a humane man," returned the doctor with a sneer, "and so my feelings may surprise you, Master Silver. But if I were sure they were raving—as I am morally certain one, at least, of them is down with fever—I should leave this camp, and at whatever risk to my own carcass, take them the assistance of my skill."

"Ask your pardon, sir, you would be very wrong," quoth Silver. "You would lose your precious life, and you may lay to that. I'm on your side now, hand and glove; and I shouldn't wish for to see the party weakened, let alone yourself, seeing as I know what I owes you. But these men down there, they couldn't keep their word—no, not supposing they wished to; and what's more, they couldn't believe as you could."

"No," said the doctor. "You're the man to keep your word, we know that."

Well, that was about the last news we had of the three pirates. Only once we heard a gunshot a great way off and supposed them to be hunting. A council was held, and it was decided that we must desert them on the island—to the huge glee, I must say, of Ben Gunn, and with the strong approval of Gray. We left a good stock of powder and shot, the bulk of the salt goat, a few medicines, and some other necessaries, tools, clothing, a spare sail, a fathom or two of rope, and by the particular desire of the doctor, a handsome present of tobacco.

That was about our last doing on the island. Before that, we had got the treasure stowed and had shipped enough water and the remainder of the goat meat in case of any distress; and at last, one fine morning, we weighed anchor, which was about all that we could manage, and stood out of North Inlet, the same colours flying that the captain had flown and fought under at the palisade.

The three fellows must have been watching us closer than we thought for, as we soon had proved. For coming through the narrows, we had to lie very near the southern point, and there we saw all three of them kneeling together on a spit of sand, with their arms raised in supplication. It went to all our hearts, I think, to leave them in that wretched state; but we could not risk another mutiny; and to take them home for the gibbet would have been a cruel sort of kindness. The doctor hailed them and told them of the stores we had left, and where they were to find them. But they continued to call us by name and appeal to us, for God's sake, to be merciful and not leave them to die in such a place.

At last, seeing the ship still bore on her course and was now swiftly drawing out of earshot, one of them—I know not which it was—leapt to his feet with a hoarse cry, whipped his musket to his shoulder, and sent a shot whistling over Silver's head and through the main-sail.

After that, we kept under cover of the bulwarks, and when next I looked out they had disappeared from the spit, and the spit itself had almost melted out of sight in the growing distance. That was, at least, the end of that; and before noon, to my inexpressible joy, the highest rock of Treasure Island had sunk into the blue round of sea.

We were so short of men that everyone on board had to bear a hand—only the captain lying on a mattress in the stern and giving his orders, for though greatly recovered he was still in want of quiet. We laid her head for the nearest port in Spanish America, for we could not risk the voyage home without fresh hands; and as it was, what with baffling winds and a couple of fresh gales, we were all worn out before we reached it.

It was just at sundown when we cast anchor in a most beautiful land-locked gulf, and were immediately surrounded by shore boats full of Negroes and Mexican Indians and half-bloods selling fruits and vegetables and offering to dive for bits of money. The sight of so many good-humoured faces (especially the blacks), the taste of the tropical fruits, and above all the lights that began to shine in the town made a most charming contrast to our dark and bloody sojourn on the island; and the doctor and the squire, taking me along with them, went ashore to pass the early part of the night. Here they met the captain of an English man-of-war, fell in talk with him, went on board his ship, and, in short, had so agreeable a time that day was breaking when we came alongside the *Hispaniola*.

Ben Gunn was on deck alone, and as soon as we came on board he began, with wonderful contortions, to make us a confession. Silver was gone. The maroon had connived at his escape in a shore boat some hours ago, and he now assured us he had only done so to preserve our lives, which would certainly have been forfeit if "that man with the one leg had stayed aboard." But this was not all. The sea-cook had not gone empty-handed. He had cut through a bulkhead unobserved and had removed one of the sacks of coin, worth perhaps three or four hundred guineas, to help him on his further wanderings.

I think we were all pleased to be so cheaply quit of him.

Well, to make a long story short, we got a few hands on board, made a good cruise home, and the

Hispaniola reached Bristol just as Mr. Blandly was beginning to think of fitting out her consort. Five men only of those who had sailed returned with her. "Drink and the devil had done for the rest," with a vengeance, although, to be sure, we were not quite in so bad a case as that other ship they sang about:

> With one man of her crew alive,
> What put to sea with seventy-five.

All of us had an ample share of the treasure and used it wisely or foolishly, according to our natures. Captain Smollett is now retired from the sea. Gray not only saved his money, but being suddenly smit with the desire to rise, also studied his profession, and he is now mate and part owner of a fine full-rigged ship, married besides, and the father of a family. As for Ben Gunn, he got a thousand pounds, which he spent or lost in three weeks, or to be more exact, in nineteen days, for he was back begging on the twentieth. Then he was given a lodge to keep, exactly as he had feared upon the island; and he still lives, a great favourite, though something of a butt, with the country boys, and a notable singer in church on Sundays and saints' days.

Of Silver we have heard no more. That formidable seafaring man with one leg has at last gone clean out of my life; but I dare say he met his old Negress, and perhaps still lives in comfort with her and Captain

Flint. It is to be hoped so, I suppose, for his chances of comfort in another world are very small.

The bar silver and the arms still lie, for all that I know, where Flint buried them; and certainly they shall lie there for me. Oxen and wain-ropes would not bring me back again to that accursed island; and the worst dreams that ever I have are when I hear the surf booming about its coasts or start upright in bed with the sharp voice of Captain Flint still ringing in my ears: "Pieces of eight! Pieces of eight!"

A Perilous Voyage

[DANIEL DEFOE]

The chief things I was employed in, besides my yearly labor of planting my barley and rice, and curing my raisins, of both which I always kept up just enough to have sufficient stock of one year's provisions beforehand—and my daily labor of going out with my gun, I had one labor, to make me a canoe, which at last I finished; so that by digging a canal to it of six feet wide, and four feet deep, I brought it into the creek, almost half a mile. As for the first, which was so vastly big, as I made it without considering beforehand, as I ought to do, how I should be able to launch it; so, never being able to bring it to the water, or bring the water to it, I was obliged to let it lie where it was, as a memorandum to teach me to be wiser next time. Indeed, the next time, though I could not get a tree proper for it, and in a place where I could not get the water to it at any less distance than, as I have said, near half a mile, yet as I saw it was practicable at last, I never gave it over; and though I was near two years about it, yet I never grudged my labor, in hopes of having a boat to go off to sea at last.

However, though my little *periagua* was finished, yet the size of it was not at all answerable to the design which I had in view when I made the first; I mean, of venturing over to the *terra firma*, where it was above forty miles broad. Accordingly, the smallness of my boat assisted to put an end to that design, and now I thought no more of it. But as I had a boat, my next design was to make a tour round the island; for as I had been on the other side in one place, crossing, as I have already described it, over the land, so the discoveries I made in that little journey made me very eager to see other parts of the coast; and now I had a boat, I thought of nothing but sailing round the island.

For this purpose, that I might do everything with discretion and consideration, I fitted up a little mast to my boat, and made a sail to it out of some of the piece of the ship's sail, which lay in store, and of which I had a great stock.

Having fitted my mast and sail, and tried the boat, I found she would sail very well. Then I made little lockers, or boxes, at either end of my boat, to put provisions, necessaries, and ammunition, etc., into, to be kept dry, either from rain or the spray of the sea; and a little long hollow place I cut in the inside of the boat, where I could lay my gun, making a flap to hang down over it to keep it dry.

I fixed my umbrella also in a step at the stern, like a mast, to stand over my head, and keep the heat of the sun off of me, like an awning; and thus I every now and then took a little voyage upon the sea, but never went far out, nor far from the little creek. But at last, being eager to view the circumference of my little kingdom, I resolved upon my tour; and accordingly I victualled my ship for the voyage, putting in two dozen of my loaves (cakes I should rather call them) of barley bread, an earthen pot full of parched rice, a food I ate a great deal of, a little bottle of rum, half a goat, and powder and shot for killing more, and two large watch-coats, of those which, as I mentioned before, I had saved out of the seamen's chests; these I took, one to lie upon, and the other to cover me in the night.

It was the 6th of November, in the sixth year of my reign, or my captivity, which you please, that I set out on this voyage, and I found it much longer than I expected; for though the island itself was not very large, yet when I came to the east side of it I found a great ledge of rocks lie out about two leagues into the sea, some above water, some under it, and beyond that a shoal of sand, lying dry half a league more; so that I was obliged to go a great way out to sea to double the point.

When first I discovered them, I was going to give over my enterprise, and come back again, not knowing how far it might oblige me to go out to sea, and, above all, doubting how I should get back again, so I came to an anchor; for I had made me a kind of anchor with a piece of a broken grappling which I got out of the ship.

Having secured my boat, I took my gun and went on shore, climbing up upon a hill, which seemed to overlook that point, where I saw the full extent of it, and resolved to venture.

In my viewing the sea from that hill, where I stood, I perceived a strong, and indeed a most furious current, which ran to the east, and even came close to the point; and I took the more notice of it, because I saw there might be some danger that when I came into it I might be carried out to sea by the strength of it, and not be able to make the island again. And indeed, had I not gotten first up upon this hill, I believe it would have been so; for there was the same current on the other side of the island, only that it set off at a farther distance; and I saw there was a strong eddy under the shore; so I had nothing to do but to get in out of the first current, and I should presently be in an eddy.

I lay here, however, two days; because the wind, blowing pretty fresh at E.S.E., and that being just contrary to the said current, made a great breach of the sea upon the point; so that it was not safe for me to keep too close to the shore for the breach, nor to go too far off because of the stream.

The third day, in the morning, the wind having abated overnight, the sea was calm, and I ventured. But I am a warning-piece again to all rash and ignorant pilots; for no sooner was I come to the point, when even I was not my boat's length from the shore, but I found myself in a great depth of water, and a current like the sluice of a mill. It carried my boat along with it with such violence, that all I could do could not keep her so much as on the edge of it, but I found it hurried me farther and farther out from the eddy, which was on my left hand. There was no wind stirring to help me, and all I could do with my paddlers signified nothing. And now I began to give myself over for lost; for, as the current was on both sides the island, I knew in a few leagues' distance they must join again, and then I was irrevocably gone. Nor did I see any possibility of avoiding it; so that I had no prospect before me but of perishing; not by the sea, for that was calm enough, but of starving for hunger. I had indeed found a tortoise on the shore, as big almost as I could lift, and had tossed it into the boat; and I had a great jar of fresh water, that is to say, one of my earthen pots; but what was all this to being driven into the vast ocean, where, to be sure, there was no shore, no mainland or island, for a thousand leagues at least.

And now I saw how easy it was for the providence of God to make the most miserable condition mankind could be in worse. Now I looked back upon my desolate solitary island as the most pleasant place in the world, and all the happiness my heart could wish for was to be but there again. I stretched out my hands to it, with eager wishes. "O happy desert!" said I, "I shall never see thee more. O miserable creature," said I, "whither am I going?" Then I reproached myself with my unthankful temper, and how I had repined at my solitary condition; and now what would I give to be on shore there again. Thus we never see the true state of our condition till it is illustrated to us by its contraries, nor know how to value what we enjoy, but by the want of it. It is scarce possible to imagine the consternation I was now in, being driven from my beloved island (for so it appeared to me now to be) into the wide ocean, almost two leagues, and in the utmost despair of ever recovering it again. However, I worked hard, till indeed my strength was almost exhausted, and kept my boat as much to the northward, that is, towards the side of the current which the eddy lay on, as possibly I could; when about noon, as the sun passed the meridian, I thought I felt a little breeze of wind in my face, springing up from the S.S.E. This cheered my heart a little, and especially when, in about half an hour more, it blew a pretty small gentle gale. By this time I was gotten at a frightful distance from the island; and had the least cloud or hazy weather intervened, I had been undone another way too; for I had no compass on board, and should never have known how to have steered towards the island if I had but once lost sight of it. But the weather continuing clear, I applied myself to get up my mast again, and spread my sail, standing away to the north as much as possible, to get out of the current.

Just as I had set my mast and sail, and the boat began to stretch away, I saw even by the clearness of the water some alteration of the current was near; for where the current was so strong, the water was foul. But perceiving the water clear, I found the current abate, and presently I found to the east, at about half a mile, a breach of the sea upon some rocks. These rocks I found caused the current to part again; and as the main stress of it ran away more southerly, leaving the rocks to the north-east, so the other returned by the repulse of the rocks, and made a strong eddy, which ran back again to the north-west with a very sharp stream.

They who know what it is to have a reprieve brought to them upon the ladder, or to be rescued from thieves just going to murder them, or who have been in such like extremities, may guess what my present surprise of joy was, and how gladly I put my boat into the stream of this eddy; and the wind also freshening, how gladly I spread my sail to it, running cheerfully before the wind, and with a strong tide or eddy under foot.

This eddy carried me about a league in my way back again, directly towards the island, but about two leagues more to the northward than the current which carried me away at first; so that when I came near the island, I found myself open to the northern shore of it, that is to say, the outer end of the island, opposite to that which I went out from.

When I had made something more than a league of way by the help of this current or eddy, I found it was spent, and served me no farther. However, I found that being between the two great currents, viz., that on the south side, which had hurried me away, and that on the north, which lay about a league on the other side; I say, between these two, in the wake of the island, I found the water at least still, and running no way; and having still a breeze of wind fair for me, I kept on steering directly for the island, though not making such fresh way as I did before.

About four o'clock in the evening, being then within about a league of the island, I found the point of the rocks which occasioned this disaster stretching out, as is described before, to the southward, and casting off the current more southwardly had, of course, made another eddy to the north, and this I found very strong, but not directly setting the way my course lay, which was due west, but almost full north. However, having a fresh gale, I stretched across this eddy, slanting north-west; and in about an hour came within about a mile of the shore, where, it being smooth water, I soon got to land.

When I was on shore, I fell on my knees, and gave God thanks for my deliverance, resolving to lay aside all thoughts of my deliverance by my boat; and refreshing myself with such things as I had, I brought my boat close to the shore, in a little cove that I had spied under some trees, and laid me down to sleep, being quite spent with the labor and fatigue of the voyage.

Storm Waves

[DOUGLAS WILSON JOHNSON]

T he enormous pressures of ocean waves are capable of producing remarkable results. Stevenson describes an instance in which a block of stone weighing 7½ tons and situated 20 feet above sea level was driven before the waves for a distance of 73 feet over rugged ledges. At North Beach, Florida, a solid block of concrete weighing 4500 lbs. was moved 12 feet horizontally and turned over on its side, while a second block weighing 3600 lbs. and having its center at high-water level was shifted several inches by waves which were not over 4 feet high. During a severe storm on December 25, 1836, stones forming part of the breakwater at Cherbourg and weighing nearly 7000 lbs. were thrown over a wall 20 feet high which surmounts the stone embankment. In the harbor of Cette a block of concrete

2500 cubic feet in volume and weighing about 125 tons was shifted more than 30 feet from its original position. Perhaps the most wonderful example of wave work is that accomplished by ocean storm waves upon the breakwater at Wick in December, 1872, and described in Stevenson's treatise on "Harbors." The seaward end of this breakwater was protected by a monolithic block of cement rubble 45 feet long, 26 feet wide and 11 feet thick, and weighing more than 800 tons, resting on great iron rods 3½ inches in diameter running through holes in the stones and embedded in the cement rubble. The entire mass, weighing 1350 tons, was torn from its place by the waves and dropped inside the pier, where it was found unbroken after the storm subsided. A much larger mass of concrete was substituted for the one removed, the new block having a volume of 1500 cubic yards, and weighing 2600 tons. In 1877 this enormous mass was similarly carried away by the waves.

The terrific impact which a wave may deliver against the face of a vertical wall may be appreciated from the fact that the facing stones of the Wick breakwater, having the same density as granite, were shattered by the sea in February, 1872. At Dunkirk waves from the narrow southern arm of the North Sea strike the coast with an impact which causes a trembling of the ground more than a mile inland. That waves have the power to wrench from place objects situated well above the main body of the wave is shown by the effects of a storm upon Dhuheartach lighthouse on the west coast of Scotland, during which fourteen stones weighing 2 tons each were torn from their positions 37 feet above high tide, and dropped into deep water. Cast-iron lamp posts on the pier heads at Duluth, located 19 feet above lake level, have repeatedly been broken off by wave action.

The lifting power of waves is often illustrated by damage to harbor works. At North Beach, Florida, a block of concrete weighing 10½ tons was lifted vertically upward three inches by the wave pressure transmitted through crevices below the mass. During a storm on Lake Superior a mass of trap rock 2 cubic yards in volume and weighing about 4½ tons was raised by a wave from its place alongside an old breakwater in Duluth and deposited on the surface of the breakwater some 5 or 6 feet above its original position. A more striking example occurred at Ymuiden on the coast of Holland, when a concrete block weighing 20 tons was lifted 12 feet vertically by a wave and deposited on a pier above high-water level.

Waves deflected upward by a sloping surface may accomplish work at high levels. The keeper of Trinidad Head light station, on the Pacific Coast, reports that during the storm of December 28, 1913, the waves repeatedly washed over Pilot rock, 103 feet high. One unusually large wave struck the cliffs below the light and rose as a solid sea apparently to the same level at which he was standing in the lantern, 196 feet above mean high water, the spray rising 25 feet or more higher. The shock of the impact against the cliffs and tower was terrific, and stopped the revolving of the light. Lake Superior waves reached the door of a light-keeper's dwelling situated 140 feet back from the water and 60½ feet above it, carrying away a board walk and doing other minor damage. On the Bound Skerry in the Shetland Islands blocks of stone from 6 to 13 tons in weight have been forced from their places at a level which is 70 to 75 feet above the sea.

The destructive power of the masses of water hurled to remarkable heights by breaking waves is greater than one might suppose. At the Bell Rock lighthouse in the North Sea a ground swell, without the aid of wind, drove water to the summit of the tower 106 feet above high tide, and broke off a ladder at an elevation of 86 feet. A bell weighing 3 cwt. was broken from its place in the Bishop Rock lighthouse, 100 feet above high-water mark, during a gale in 1860; and at Unst, in the Shetland Islands, a door was broken open at a height of 195 feet above the sea. The keeper of Tillamook Rock lighthouse, on the coast of Oregon, reports that in the winter of

1902 the water of the waves was thrown more than 200 feet above the level of the sea, descending upon the roof of his house in apparently solid masses. In October 1912, and again in November 1913, the panes of plate glass in the lantern of this same light, 132 feet above mean high water, were broken in by storm waves.

Great damage may be accomplished by the falling water. According to Shield "it is no uncommon occurrence for storm waves, striking a vertical breakwater face, to throw heavy masses of water to a height of at least 100 feet, often very much higher. Such water in its descent on reaching the roadway of the breakwater upon which it falls, will have attained a velocity of about 80 feet per second, or nearly double the velocity and four times the force of the water striking the face of the breakwater." During a severe gale at Buffalo in December, 1899, seventy big timbers, 12 x 12 inches in thickness, 12 feet long, and 10 feet between supports, were broken in two in the middle by the impact of the falling water. This same breakwater was further damaged a year later when waves breaking against it were hurled from 75 to 125 feet into the air, the falling water crushing the big timbers on which it fell as though they had been pipe-stems.

A part of the geological work accomplished by waves is due to the direct pressure exerted upon air and water imprisoned in crevices, and another part to the sudden expansion of air in crevices and pore spaces when the rapid retreat of a wave creates a partial vacuum outside. The effect of compressed air may be inferred from the fact that waves coming against a breakwater in Buffalo harbor produced such high pressure upon the air under the concrete shell that four circular plates of concrete, 3 feet in diameter, 6 inches thick and weighing 530 lbs. each, serving as covers to manholes, were lifted from their places. A block weighing 7 tons in the face of the breakwater at Ymuiden was started forward out of its place during a gale, the movement being *toward* the waves which were coming against it. According to Gaillard this phenomenon was caused "by the stroke of a wave compressing the air in the rear of it" but similar results are produced by expansion due to the formation of a partial vacuum in front. In 1840 a securely fastened door in the Eddystone lighthouse was burst *outward* during the attack of storm waves, the circumstances leading Geikie to conclude that "by sudden sinking of a mass of water hurled against the building, a partial vacuum was formed, and the air inside forced out the door in its efforts to restore the equilibrium."

Another important factor in the work of waves is the effect produced by stones, logs, blocks of ice, and other objects moving with the waves. It has been well said by Platfair that waves thus armed become a sort of "powerful artillery" with which the ocean assails the land. A large block of ice or a log may concentrate its whole momentum upon a very small area with appropriately great results. Thus, Gaillard has suggested that an exceptionally high dynamometer reading on Lake Michigan (when the instrument showed a pressure twice as great as that recorded in the same locality for a more severe storm and greater than any record for the larger waves of Lake Superior) may possibly have been caused by ice or timber. Large stones may be hurled out of the water with high velocities. At Tillamook Rock on the Oregon Coast, fragments of stones are torn from the cliffs during every severe storm and thrown on the roof of the light-keeper's house, about 100 feet above sea level. "In December, 1894, one fragment weighing 135 lbs. was thrown clear above this building, and in falling broke a hole 20 feet square through the roof, practically wrecking the interior of the building. Thirteen panes of glass in the lantern were broken during the same storm." As already noted, this lantern is 132 feet above mean high water. The fog-signal siren horns, about 95 feet above the sea, were partially filled with rocks during the storm of October 18, 1912. The windows of the Dunnet

Head lighthouse on the north coast of Scotland, which are over 300 feet above high-water mark, are sometimes broken by stones swept up the cliffs by waves.

It is perfectly evident that waves which are armed with cobblestones and enormous boulders must accomplish great erosive work when they beat against a cliff or artificial wall. On the other hand, one must not make the mistake of assuming that waves which are not thus armed can accomplish but little work. It is true that large storm waves may beat against a cliff without removing the barnacles which are attached to its face, and that along the shores of saline lakes calcareous tufa may form on cliffs exposed to the impact of large waves. But this merely indicates that the pressure of the liquid mass is so evenly distributed upon all sides of the strong shell, or of the mineral deposit, that the excess of pressure on any one side is not sufficiently great nor applied with sufficient suddenness to cause rupture. The same waves will wrench great blocks of rock from their places in the cliff face, and drive air and water into joint crevices with such force as to loosen large fragments of the cliff and thus contribute to the disintegration of the whole mass. A force which exerts a pressure of thousands of pounds to the square foot will discover lines of weakness in any natural cliff. Even though all sand, boulders, and other rock fragments were speedily carried out of the zone of wave action, and waves of pure water alone attacked the coasts, shore-lines would retreat under wave erosion just as surely as they do when the waves are armed with abrasive materials, although the process would certainly go on much more slowly.

An Imprisoned Thunderstorm

[VICTOR HUGO]

The captain and lieutenant rushed towards the gun-deck, but could not get down. All the gunners were pouring up in dismay. Something terrible had just happened.

One of the carronades of the battery, a twenty-four pounder, had broken loose.

This is the most dangerous accident that can possibly take place on shipboard. Nothing more terrible can happen to a sloop of war in open sea and under full sail.

A cannon that breaks its moorings suddenly becomes some strange, supernatural beast. It is a machine transformed into a monster. That short mass on wheels moves like a billiard-ball, rolls with the rolling of the ship, plunges with the pitching, goes, comes, stops, seems to meditate, starts on its course again, shoots like an arrow, from one end of the vessel to the other, whirls around, slips away, dodges, rears, bangs, crashes, kills, exterminates. It is a battering ram capriciously assaulting a wall. Add to this, the fact that the ram is of metal, the wall of wood.

It is matter set free; one might say, this eternal slave was avenging itself; it seems as if the total depravity concealed in what we call inanimate things had escaped, and burst forth all of a sudden; it appears to lose patience, and to take a strange mysterious revenge; nothing more relentless than this wrath of the inanimate. This enraged lump leaps like a panther, it has the clumsiness of an elephant, the nimbleness of a mouse, the obstinacy of an ax, the uncertainty of the billows, the zigzag of the lightening, the deafness of the grave. It weighs ten thousand pounds, and it rebounds like a child's ball. It spins and then abruptly darts off at right angles.

And what is to be done? How put an end to it? A tempest ceases, a cyclone passes over, a wind dies down, a broken mast can be replaced, a leak can be stopped, a fire extinguished, but what will become of this enormous brute of bronze? How can it be captured? You can reason with a bulldog, astonish a bull, fascinate a boa, frighten a tiger, tame a lion; but you have no resource against this monster, a loose cannon. You cannot kill it, it is dead; and at the same time it lives. It lives with a sinister life which comes to it from the infinite. The deck beneath it gives it full swing. It is moved by the ship, which is moved by the sea, which is moved by the wind. This destroyer is a toy. The ship, the waves, the winds, all play with it, hence its frightful animation. What is to be done with this apparatus? How fetter this stupendous engine of destruction? How anticipate its comings and goings, its returns, its stops, its shocks? Any one of its blows on the side of the ship may stave it in. How fortell its frightful meanderings? It is dealing with a projectile, which alters its mind, which seems to have ideas, and changes its direction every instant. How check the course of what must be avoided? The horrible cannon struggles, advances, backs, strikes right, strikes left, retreats, passes by, disconcerts expectation, grinds up obstacles, crushes men like flies. All the terror of the situation is in the fluctuations of the flooring. How fight an inclined plane subject to caprices? The ship has, so to speak, in its belly, an imprisoned thunderstorm, striving to escape; something like a thunderbolt rumbling above an earthquake.

In an instant the whole crew was on foot. It was the fault of the gun captain, who had neglected to fasten the screw-nut of the mooring-chain, and had insecurely clogged the four wheels of the gun carriage; this gave play to the sole and the framework, separated the two platforms, and finally the breeching. The tackle had given way, so that the cannon was no longer firm on its carriage. The stationary breeching, which prevents recoil, was not in use at this time. A heavy sea struck the port, the carronade insecurely fastened, had recoiled and broken its chain, and began its terrible course over the deck.

To form an idea of this strange sliding, let one image a drop of water running over glass.

At the moment when the fastenings gave way, the gunners were in the battery. Some in groups, others scattered about, busied with the customary work among sailors getting ready for a signal for action. The carronade, hurled forward by the pitching of the vessel, made a gap in this crowd of men and crushed four at the first blow; then sliding back and shot out again as the ship rolled, it cut in two a fifth unfortunate, and knocked a piece of the battery against the larboard side with such force as to unship it. This caused the cry of distress just heard. All the men rushed to the companion-way. The gun deck was vacated in a twinkling.

The enormous gun was left alone. It was given up to itself. It was its own master, and master of the ship. It could do what it pleased. This whole crew, accustomed to laugh in time of battle, now trembled. To describe the terror is impossible.

Captain Boisberthelot and Lieutenant la Vieuville, although both dauntless men, stopped at the head of the companion-way and dumb, pale, and hesitating, looked down on the deck below. Someone elbowed past and went down.

It was their passenger, the peasant, the man of whom they had just been speaking a moment before.

Reaching the foot of the companion-way, he stopped.

The cannon was rushing back and forth on the deck. One might have supposed it to be the living chariot of the Apocalypse. The marine lantern swinging overhead added a dizzy shifting of light and shade to the picture. The form of the cannon disappeared in the violence of its course, and it looked now black in the light, now mysteriously white in the darkness.

It went on in its destructive work. It had already shattered four other guns and made two gaps in the side of the ship, fortunately above the water-line, but where the water would come in, in case of heavy weather. It rushed frantically against the framework; the strong timbers withstood the shock; the curved shape of the wood gave them great power of resistance; but they creaked beneath the blows of this huge club, beating on all sides at once, with a strange sort of ubiquity. The percussions of a grain of shot shaken in a bottle are not swifter or more senseless. The four wheels passed back and forth over the dead men, cutting them, carving them, slashing them, till the five corpses were a score of stumps rolling across the deck; the heads of the dead men seemed to cry out; streams of blood curled over the deck with the rolling of the vessel; the planks, damaged in several places, began to gape open. The whole ship was filled with the horrid noise and confusion.

The captain promptly recovered his presence of mind and ordered everything that could check and impede the cannon's mad course to be thrown through the hatchway down on the gun deck—mattresses, hammocks, spare sails, rolls of cordage, bags belonging to the crew, and bales of counterfeit assignats, of which the corvette carried a large quantity—a characteristic piece of English villainy regarded as legitimate warfare.

But what could these rags do? As nobody dared to go below to dispose of them properly, they were reduced to lint in a few minutes.

There was just sea enough to make the accident as bad as possible. A tempest would have been desirable, for it might have upset the cannon, and with its four wheels once in the air there would be some hope of getting it under control. Meanwhile, the havoc increased.

There were splits and fractures in the masts, which are set into the framework of the keel and rise above the decks of ships like great, round pillars. The convulsive blows of the cannon had cracked the mizzen-mast, and had cut into the main-mast.

The battery was being ruined. Ten pieces out of thirty were disabled; the breaches in the side of the vessel were increasing, and the corvette was beginning to leak.

The old passenger, having gone down to the gun deck, stood like a man of stone at the foot of the steps. He cast a stern glance over this scene of devastation. He did not move. It seemed impossible to take a step forward. Every movement of the loose carronade threatened the ship's destruction. A few moments more and shipwreck would be inevitable.

They must perish or put a speedy end to the disaster; some course must be decided on; but what? What an opponent was this carronade! Something must be done to stop this terrible madness—to capture this lightning—to overthrow this thunderbolt.

Boisberthelot said to La Vieuville,—

"Do you believe in God, chevalier?"

La Vieuville replied: "Yes—no. Sometimes."

"During a tempest."

"Yes, and in moments like this."

"God alone can save us from this," said Boisberthelot.

Everybody was silent, letting the carronade continue its horrible din.

Outside, the waves beating against the ship responded with their blows to the shocks of the cannon. It was like two hammers alternating.

Suddenly, in the midst of this inaccessible ring, where the escaped cannon was leaping, a man was seen to appear, with an iron bar in his hand. He was the author of the catastrophe, the captain of the gun, guilty of criminal carelessness, and the cause of the accident, the master of the carronade. Having done the mischief, he was anxious to repair it. He had seized the iron bar in one hand, a tiller-rope with a slip-noose in the other, and jumped down the hatchway to the gun deck.

Then began an awful sight; a Titanic scene; the contest between gun and gunner; the battle of matter and intelligence, the duel between man and the inanimate.

The man stationed himself in a corner, and with bar and rope in his two hands, he leaned against one of the riders, braced himself on his legs, which seemed two steel posts, and livid, calm, tragic, as if rooted to the deck, he waited.

He waited for the cannon to pass by him.

The gunner knew his gun, and it seemed to him as if the gun ought to know him. He had lived long with it. How many times he had thrust his hand into its mouth! It was his own familiar master. He began to speak to it as if it were his dog.

"Come!" he said. Perhaps he loved it.

He seemed to wish it to come to him.

But to come to him was to come upon him. And then he would be lost. How could he avoid being crushed? That was the question. All looked on in terror.

Not a breast breathed freely, unless perhaps that of the old man, who was alone in the battery with the two contestants, a stern witness.

He might be crushed himself by the cannon. He did not stir.

Beneath them the sea blindly directed the contest.

At the moment when the gunner, accepting this frightful hand-to-hand conflict, challenged the cannon, some chance rocking of the sea caused the carronade to remain for an instant motionless and as if stupefied. "Come, now!" said the man. It seemed to listen.

Suddenly it leaped towards him. The man dodged the blow.

The battle began. Battle unprecedented. Frailty struggling against the invulnerable. The gladiator of flesh attacking the beast of brass. On one side, brute, force; on the other, a human soul.

All of this was taking place in semi-darkness. It was like the shadowy vision of a miracle.

A soul—strange to say, one would have thought the cannon also had a soul; but a soul full of hatred and rage. This sightless thing seemed to have eyes. The monster appeared to lie in wait for the man. One would have at least believed that there was craft in this mass. It also chose its time. It was a strange, gigantic insect of metal, having or seeming to have the will of a demon. For a moment this colossal locust would beat against the low ceiling overhead, then it would come down on its four wheels like a tiger on its four paws, and begin to run at the man. He, supple, nimble, expert, writhed away like an adder from all these lightening movements. He avoided a collision, but the blows which he parried fell against the vessel, and continued their work of destruction.

An end of broken chain was left hanging to the carronade. This chain had in some way become twisted about the crew of the cascabel. One end of the chain was fastened to the gun-carriage. The other, left loose, whirled desperately about the cannon, making all its blows more dangerous.

The screw held it in a firm grip, adding a thong to a battering-ram, making a terrible whirlwind around the cannon, an iron lash in a brazen hand. This chain complicated the contest.

However, the man went on fighting. Occasionally, it was the man who attacked the cannon; he would creep along the side of the vessel, bar and rope in hand; and the cannon, as if it understood, and as though suspecting some snare, would flee away. The man, bent on victory, pursued it.

Such things cannot long continue. The cannon seemed to say to itself, all of a sudden, "Come, now! Make an end of it!" and it stopped. One felt that the crisis was at hand. The cannon, as if in suspense, seemed to have, or really had—for to all it was a living being—a ferocious malice prepense. It made a sudden, quick dash at the gunner. The gunner sprang out of the way, let it pass by, and cried out to it with a laugh, "Try it again!" The cannon, as if enraged, smashed a carronade on the port side; then, again seized by the invisible sling which controlled it, it was hurled to the starboard side at the man, who made his escape. Three carronades gave way under the blows of the cannon; then, as if blind and not knowing what more to do, it turned its back on the man, rolled from stern to bow, injured the stern and made a breach in the planking of the prow. The man took refuge at the foot of the steps, not far from the old man who was looking on. The gunner held his iron bar in rest. The cannon seemed to notice it, and without taking the trouble to turn around, slid back on the man, swift as the blow of an ax. The man driven against the side of the ship, was lost. The whole crew cried out with horror.

But the old passenger, till this moment motionless, darted forth more quickly than any of this wildly swift rapidity. He seized a package of counterfeit assignats, and, at the risk of being crushed, succeeded in throwing it between the wheels of the carronade. This decisive and perilous movement could not have been made with more exactness and precision by a man trained in all the exercises described in Durosel's "Manual of Gun Practice at Sea."

The package had the effect of a clog. A pebble may stop a log, the branch of a tree turn aside an avalanche. The carronade stumbled. The gunner taking advantage of the critical opportunity, plunged his iron bar between the spoke of one of the hind wheels. The cannon stopped. It leaned forward. The man using the bar as a lever, held it in equilibrium. The heavy mass was overthrown, with the crash of a falling bell, and the man, rushing with all his might, dripping with perspiration, passed the slip-noose around the bronze neck of the subdued monster.

It was ended. The man had conquered. The ant had control over the mastodon; the pigmy had taken the thunderbolt prisoner.

The mariners and sailors clapped their hands.

The whole crew rushed forward with cables and chains, and in an instant the cannon was secured.

Passage Toward New Holland

[WILLIAM BLIGH]

1789. May.

It was about eight o'clock at night when we bore away under reefed lug fore-sail and, having divided the people into watches and got the boat in a little order, we returned God thanks for our miraculous preservation and, fully confident of his gracious support, I found my mind more at ease than it had been for some time past.

Sunday 3.

At daybreak the gale increased; the sun rose very fiery and red, a sure indication of a severe gale of wind. At eight it blew a violent storm and the sea ran very high, so that between the seas the sail was becalmed, and when on the top of the sea it was too much to have set: but we could not venture to take in the sail for we were in very imminent danger and distress, the sea curling over the stern of the boat, which obliged us to bale with all our might. A situation more distressing has perhaps seldom been experienced.

Our bread was in bags and in danger of being spoiled by the wet: to be starved to death was inevitable if this could not be prevented: I therefore began to examine what clothes there were in the boat and what other things could be spared and, having determined that only two suits should be kept for each person, the rest was thrown overboard with some rope and spare sails, which lightened the boat considerably, and we had more room to bale the water out. Fortunately the carpenter had a good chest in the boat, in which we secured the bread the first favourable moment. His tool chest also was cleared and the tools stowed in the bottom of the boat so that this became a second convenience.

I served a teaspoonful of rum to each person (for we were very wet and cold) with a quarter of a breadfruit, which was scarce eatable, for dinner: our engagement was now strictly to be carried into execution, and I was fully determined to make our provisions last eight weeks, let the daily proportion be ever so small.

At noon I considered our course and distance from Tofoa to be west-north-west three-quarters west 86 miles, latitude 19 degrees 27 minutes south. I directed the course to the west-north-west that we might get a sight of the islands called Feejee if they laid in the direction the natives had pointed out to me.

The weather continued very severe, the wind veering from north-east to east-south-east. The sea ran higher than in the forenoon, and the fatigue of baling to keep the boat from filling was exceedingly great. We could do nothing more than keep before the sea, in the course of which the boat performed so well that I no longer dreaded any danger in that respect. But, among the hardships we were to undergo, that of being constantly wet was not the least.

Monday 4.

The night was very cold and at daylight our limbs were so benumbed that we could scarce find the use of them. At this time I served a teaspoonful of rum to each person, from which we all found great benefit.

As I have mentioned before I determined to keep to the west-north-west till I got more to the northward, for I not only expected to have better weather but to see the Feejee Islands, as I have often understood from the natives of Annamooka that they lie in that direction. Captain Cook likewise considered them to be north-west by west from Tongataboo. Just before noon we discovered a small flat island of a moderate height bearing west–south–west 4 or 5 leagues. I observed our latitude to be 18 degrees 58 minutes south; our longitude was by account 3 degrees 4 minutes west from the island of Tofoa, having made a north 72 degrees west course, distance 95 miles, since yesterday noon. I divided five small coconuts for our dinner and everyone was satisfied.

A little after noon other islands appeared, and at a quarter past three o'clock we could count eight, bearing from south round by the west to north–west by north, those to the south which were the nearest being four leagues distant from us.

I kept my course to the north–west by west between the islands, the gale having considerably abated. At six o'clock we discovered three other small islands to the north–west, the westernmost of them bore north–west half west 7 leagues. I steered to the southward of these islands a west–north–west course for the night under a reefed sail.

Served a few broken pieces of breadfruit for supper and performed prayers.

The night turned out fair and, having had tolerable rest, everyone seemed considerably better in the morning, and contentedly breakfasted on a few pieces of yams that were found in the boat. After breakfast we examined our bread, a great deal of which was damaged and rotten; this nevertheless we were glad to keep for use.

I had hitherto been scarcely able to keep any account of our run, but we now equipped ourselves a little better by getting a log-line marked and, having practised at counting seconds, several could do it with some degree of exactness.

The islands we had passed lie between the latitude of 19 degrees 5 minutes south and 18 degrees 19 minutes south, and according to my reckoning from 3 degrees 17 minutes to 3 degrees 46 minutes west longitude from the island Tofoa: the largest may be about six leagues in circuit; but it is impossible for me to be very correct. To show where they are to be found again is the most my situation enabled me to do. The sketch I have made will give a comparative view of their extent. I believe all the larger islands are inhabited as they appeared very fertile.

At noon I observed in latitude 18 degrees 10 seconds south and considered my course and distance from yesterday noon north-west by west half west 94 miles; longitude by account from Tofoa 4 degrees 29 minutes west.

For dinner I served some of the damaged bread and a quarter of a pint of water.

About six o'clock in the afternoon we discovered two islands, one bearing west by south 6 leagues and the other north-west by north 8 leagues; I kept to windward of the northernmost and, passing it by 10 o'clock, I resumed our course to the north-west and west-north-west for the night.

Wednesday 6.

The weather was fair and the wind moderate all day from the east-north-east. At daylight a number of other islands were in sight from south-south-east to the west and round to north-east by east; between those in the north-west I determined to pass. At noon a small sandy island or key two miles distant from me bore from east to south three-quarters west. I had passed ten islands, the largest of which I judged to be 6 or 8 leagues in circuit. Much larger lands appeared in the south-west and north-north-west, between which I directed my course. Latitude observed 17 degrees 17 minutes south; course since yesterday noon north 50 degrees west; distance 84 miles; longitude made by account 5 degrees 37 minutes west.

Our allowance for the day was a quarter of a pint of coconut milk and the meat, which did not exceed two ounces to each person: it was received very contentedly but we suffered great drought. I durst not venture to land as we had no arms and were less capable of defending ourselves than we were at Tofoa.

To keep an account of the boat's run was rendered difficult from being constantly wet with the sea breaking over us but, as we advanced towards the land, the sea became smoother and I was enabled to form a sketch of the islands which will serve to give a general knowledge of their extent and position. Those we were near appeared fruitful and hilly, some very mountainous and all of a good height.

To our great joy we hooked a fish, but we were miserably disappointed by its being lost in trying to get it into the boat.

We continued steering to the north-west between the islands which by the evening appeared of considerable extent, woody and mountainous. At sunset the southernmost bore from south to south-west by west and the northernmost from north by west half west to north-east half east. At six o'clock we were nearly midway between them and about 6 leagues distant from each shore when we fell in with a coral bank, on which we had only four feet water, without the least break on it or ruffle of the sea to give us warning. I could see that it extended about a mile on each side of us, but as it is probable that it may extend much further I have laid it down so in my sketch.

I directed the course west by north for the night, and served to each person an ounce of the damaged bread and a quarter of a pint of water for supper.

As our lodgings were very miserable and confined for want of room I endeavoured to remedy the latter defect by putting ourselves at watch and watch; so that one half always sat up while the other lay down on the boat's bottom or upon a chest, with nothing to cover us but the heavens. Our limbs were dreadfully cramped for we could not stretch them out, and the nights were so cold, and we so constantly wet, that after a few hours sleep we could scarce move.

Thursday 7.

At dawn of day we again discovered land from west-south-west to west-north-west, and another island north-north-west, the latter a high round lump of but little extent: the southern land that we had passed in the night was still in sight. Being very wet and cold I served a spoonful of rum and a morsel of bread for breakfast.

The land in the west was distinguished by some extraordinary high rocks which, as we approached them, assumed a variety of forms. The country appeared to be agreeably interspersed with high and low land, and in some places covered with wood. Off the north-east part lay some small rocky islands, between which and an island 4 leagues to the north-east I directed my course; but a lee current very unexpectedly set us very near to the rocky isles, and we could only get clear of it by rowing, passing close to the reef that surrounded them. At this time we observed two large sailing canoes coming swiftly after us along shore and, being apprehensive of their intentions, we rowed with some anxiety, fully sensible of our weak and defenceless state. At noon it was calm and the weather cloudy; my latitude is therefore doubtful to 3 or 4 miles. Our course since yesterday noon north-west by west, distance 79 miles; latitude by account 16 degrees 29 minutes south, and longitude by account from Tofoa 6 degrees 46 minutes west. Being constantly wet it was with the utmost difficulty I could open a book to write, and I am sensible that what I have done can only serve to point out where these lands are to be found again, and give an idea of their extent.

All the afternoon we had light winds at north-north-east: the weather was very rainy, attended with thunder and lightning. Only one of the canoes gained upon us, which by three o'clock in the afternoon was not more than two miles off, when she gave over chase.

If I may judge from the sail of these vessels they are of a similar construction with those at the Friendly Islands which, with the nearness of their situation, gives reason to believe that they are the same kind of people. Whether these canoes had any hostile intention against us must remain a doubt: perhaps we might have benefited by an intercourse with them, but in our defenceless situation to have made the experiment would have been risking too much.

I imagine these to be the islands called Feejee as their extent, direction, and distance from the Friendly Islands answers to the description given of them by those Islanders. Heavy rain came on at four o'clock, when every person did their utmost to catch some water, and we increased our stock to 34 gallons, besides quenching our thirst for the first time since we had been at sea; but an attendant consequence made us pass the night very miserably for, being extremely wet and having no dry things to shift or cover us, we experienced cold and shiverings scarce to be conceived. Most fortunately for us the forenoon turned out fair and we stripped and dried our clothes. The allowance I issued today was an ounce and a half of pork, a teaspoonful of rum, half a pint of coconut milk, and an ounce of bread. The rum though so small in quantity was of the greatest service. A fishing-line was generally towing from the stern of the boat but though we saw great numbers of fish we could never catch one.

At noon I observed in latitude 16 degrees 4 minutes south and found we had made a course from yesterday noon north 62 degrees west distance 62 miles; longitude by account from Tofoa 7 degrees 42 minutes west.

The land passed yesterday and the day before is a group of islands, 14 or 16 in number, lying between the latitude of 16 degrees 26 minutes south and 17 degrees 57 minutes south, and in longitude by my account 4 degrees 47 minutes to 7 degrees 17 minutes west from Tofoa. Three of these islands are very large, having from 30 to 40 leagues of sea-coast.

In the afternoon we cleaned out the boat and it employed us till sunset to get everything dry and in order. Hitherto I had issued the allowance by guess, but I now made a pair of scales with two coconut shells and, having accidentally some pistol-balls in the boat, 25 of which weighed one pound or 16 ounces, I adopted one, as the proportion of weight that each person should receive of bread at the times I served it. I also amused all hands with describing the situation of New Guinea and New Holland, and gave them every information in my power that in case any accident happened to me those who survived might have some idea of what they were about, and be able to find their way to Timor, which at present they knew nothing of more than the name and some not even that. At night I served a quarter of a pint of water and half an ounce of bread for supper.

Saturday 9.

In the morning a quarter of a pint of coconut milk and some of the decayed bread was served for breakfast, and for dinner I divided the meat of four coconuts with the remainder of the rotten bread, which was only eatable by such distressed people.

At noon I observed the latitude to be 15 degrees 47 minutes south; course since yesterday north 75 degrees west distance 64 miles; longitude made by account 8 degrees 45 minutes west.

In the afternoon I fitted a pair of shrouds for each mast, and contrived a canvas weather cloth round the boat, and raised the quarters about nine inches by nailing on the seats of the stern sheets, which proved of great benefit to us.

The wind had been moderate all day in the southeast quarter with fine weather; but about nine o'clock in the evening the clouds began to gather, and we had a prodigious fall of rain with severe thunder and lightning. By midnight we caught about twenty gallons of water. Being miserably wet and cold I served to the people a teaspoonful of rum each to enable them to bear with their distressed situation. The weather continued extremely bad and the wind increased; we spent a very miserable night without sleep except such as could be got in the midst of rain. The day brought no relief but its light. The sea broke over us so much that two men were constantly baling; and we had no choice how to steer, being obliged to keep before the waves for fear of the boat filling.

The allowance now regularly served to each person was one 25th of a pound of bread and a quarter of a pint of water, at eight in the morning, at noon, and at sunset. Today I gave about half an ounce of pork for dinner which, though any moderate person would have considered only as a mouthful, was divided into three or four.

The rain abated towards noon and I observed the latitude to be 15 degrees 17 minutes south; course north 67 degrees west distance 78 miles; longitude made 10 degrees west.

The wind continued strong from south-south-east to south-east with very squally weather and a high breaking sea, so that we were miserably wet and suffered great cold in the night.

Monday 11.

In the morning at daybreak I served to every person a teaspoonful of rum, our limbs being so cramped that we could scarce move them. Our situation was now extremely dangerous, the sea frequently running over our stern, which kept us baling with all our strength.

At noon the sun appeared, which gave us as much pleasure as in a winter's day in England. I issued the 25th of a pound of bread and a quarter of a pint of water, as yesterday. Latitude observed 14 degrees 50 minutes south; course north 71 degrees west distance 102 miles; and longitude by account 11 degrees 39 minutes west from Tofoa.

In the evening it rained hard and we again experienced a dreadful night.

Tuesday 12.

At length the day came and showed to me a miserable set of beings, full of wants, without anything to relieve them. Some complained of great pain in their bowels, and everyone of having almost lost the use of his limbs. The little sleep we got was no ways refreshing as we were covered with sea and rain. I served a spoonful of rum at day-dawn, and the usual allowance of bread and water for breakfast, dinner, and supper.

At noon it was almost calm, no sun to be seen, and some of us shivering with cold. Course since yesterday west by north distance 89 miles; latitude by account 14 degrees 33 minutes south; longitude made 13 degrees 9 minutes west. The direction of our course was to pass to the northward of the New Hebrides.

The wet weather continued and in the afternoon the wind came from the southward, blowing fresh in squalls. As there was no prospect of getting our clothes dried I recommended to everyone to strip and wring them through the salt water, by which means they received a warmth that while wet with rain they could not have.

This afternoon we saw a kind of fruit on the water which Nelson told me was the Barringtonia of Forster and, as I saw the same again in the morning, and some men-of-war birds, I was led to believe that we were not far from land.

We continued constantly shipping seas and baling, and were very wet and cold in the night; but I could not afford the allowance of rum at daybreak.

Wednesday 13.

At noon I had a sight of the sun, latitude 14 degrees 17 minutes south. Course west by north 79 miles; longitude made 14 degrees 28 minutes west. All this day we were constantly shipping water and suffered much cold and shiverings in the night.

Thursday 14.

Fresh gales at south-east and gloomy weather with rain and a high sea. At six in the morning we saw land from south-west by south eight leagues to north-west by west three-quarters west six leagues, which soon after appeared to be four islands, one of them much larger than the others, and all of them high and remarkable. At noon we discovered a small island and some rocks bearing north-west by north four leagues, and another island west eight leagues, so that the whole were six in number; the four I had first seen bearing from south half east to south-west by south; our distance three leagues from the nearest island. My latitude observed was 13 degrees 29 minutes south, and longitude by account from Tofoa 15 degrees 49 minutes west; course since yesterday noon north 63 degrees west distance 89 miles. At four in the afternoon we passed the westernmost island.

Friday 15.

At one in the morning another island was discovered bearing west-north-west five leagues distance, and at eight o'clock we saw it for the last time bearing north-east seven leagues. A number of gannets, boobies, and men-of-war birds were seen.

These islands lie between the latitude of 13 degrees 16 minutes and 14 degrees 10 minutes south: their longitude according to my reckoning 15 degrees 51 minutes to 17 degrees 6 minutes west from the island Tofoa. The largest island I judged to be about twenty leagues in circuit, the others five or six. The easternmost is the smallest island and most remarkable, having a high sugar loaf hill.

The sight of these islands served only to increase the misery of our situation. We were very little better than starving with plenty in view; yet to attempt procuring any relief was attended with so much danger that prolonging of life, even in the midst of misery, was thought preferable, while there remained hopes of being able to surmount our hardships. For my own part I consider the general run of cloudy and wet weather to be a blessing of Providence. Hot weather would have caused us to have died with thirst; and probably being so constantly covered with rain or sea protected us from that dreadful calamity.

As I had nothing to assist my memory I could not then determine whether these islands were a part of the New Hebrides or not: I believe them to be a new discovery which I have since found true but, though they were not seen either by Monsieur Bougainville or Captain Cook, they are so nearly in the neighbourhood of the New Hebrides that they must be considered as part of the same group. They are fertile and inhabited, as I saw smoke in several places.

The wind was at south-east with rainy weather all day. The night was very dark, not a star could be seen to steer by, and the sea broke continually over us. I found it necessary to counteract as much as possible the effect of the southerly winds to prevent being driven too near New Guinea, for in general we were forced to keep so much before the sea that if we had not, at intervals of moderate weather, steered a more southerly course we should inevitably from a continuance of the gales have been thrown in sight of that coast: in which case there would most probably have been an end to our voyage.

Saturday 16.

In addition to our miserable allowance of one 25th of a pound of bread and a quarter of a pint of water

I issued for dinner about an ounce of salt pork to each person. I was often solicited for this pork, but I considered it more proper to issue it in small quantities than to suffer it to be all used at once or twice, which would have been done if I had allowed it.

At noon I observed in 13 degrees 33 minutes south, longitude made from Tofoa 19 degrees 27 minutes west; course north 82 degrees west, distance 101 miles. The sun breaking out through the clouds gave us hopes of drying our wet clothes, but the sunshine was of short duration. We had strong breezes at south-east by south and dark gloomy weather with storms of thunder, lightning, and rain. The night was truly horrible, and not a star to be seen; so that our steerage was uncertain.

Sunday 17.

At dawn of day I found every person complaining, and some of them solicited extra allowance, which I positively refused. Our situation was miserable: always wet, and suffering extreme cold in the night without the least shelter from the weather. Being constantly obliged to bale to keep the boat from filling was perhaps not to be reckoned an evil as it gave us exercise.

The little rum we had was of great service: when our nights were particularly distressing I generally served a teaspoonful or two to each person: and it was always joyful tidings when they heard of my intentions.

At noon a water-spout was very near on board of us. I issued an ounce of pork in addition to the allowance of bread and water; but before we began to eat every person stripped and, having wrung their clothes through the seawater, found much warmth and refreshment. Course since yesterday noon west-south-west distance 100 miles; latitude by account 14 degrees 11 minutes south and longitude made 21 degrees 3 minutes west.

The night was dark and dismal: the sea constantly breaking over us and nothing but the wind and waves to direct our steerage. It was my intention if possible to make New Holland to the southward of Endeavour straits, being sensible that it was necessary to preserve such a situation as would make a southerly wind a fair one, that we might range along the reefs till an opening should be found into smooth water, and we the sooner be able to pick up some refreshments.

Monday 18.

In the morning the rain abated, when we stripped and wrung our clothes through the seawater as usual, which refreshed us greatly. Every person complained of violent pain in their bones; I was only surprised that no one was yet laid up. The customary allowance of one 25th of a pound of bread and a quarter of a pint of water was served at breakfast, dinner, and supper.

At noon I deduced my situation by account, for we had no glimpse of the sun, to be in latitude 14 degrees 52 minutes south; course since yesterday noon west-south-west 106 miles; longitude made from Tofoa 22 degrees 45 minutes west. Saw many boobies and noddies, a sign of being in the neighbourhood of land. In the night we had very severe lightning with heavy rain and were obliged to keep baling without intermission.

Tuesday 19.

Very bad weather and constant rain. At noon latitude by account 14 degrees 37 minutes south; course since yesterday north 81 degrees west, distance 100 miles; longitude made 24 degrees 30 minutes west. With the allowance of bread and water served half an ounce of pork to each person for dinner.

Wednesday 20.

Fresh breezes east-north-east with constant rain, at times a deluge. Always baling.

At dawn of day some of my people seemed half dead: our appearances were horrible, and I could look no way but I caught the eye of someone in distress. Extreme hunger was now too evident, but no one suffered from thirst, nor had we much inclination to drink, that desire perhaps being satisfied through the skin. The little sleep we got was in the midst of water, and we constantly awoke with severe cramps and pains in our bones. This morning I served about two teaspoonfuls of rum to each person and the allowance of bread and water as usual. At noon the sun broke out and revived everyone. I found we were in latitude 14 degrees 49 minutes south; longitude made 25 degrees 46 minutes west; course south 88 degrees west distance 75 miles.

All the afternoon we were so covered with rain and salt water that we could scarcely see. We suffered extreme cold and everyone dreaded the approach of night. Sleep, though we longed for it, afforded no comfort: for my own part I almost lived without it.

Thursday 21.

About two o'clock in the morning we were overwhelmed with a deluge of rain. It fell so heavy that we were afraid it would fill the boat, and were obliged to bale with all our might. At dawn of day I served a larger allowance of rum. Towards noon the rain abated and the sun shone, but we were miserably cold and wet, the sea breaking constantly over us so that, notwithstanding the heavy rain, we had not been able to add to our stock of fresh water. Latitude by observation 14 degrees 29 minutes south, and longitude made by account from Tofoa 27 degrees 25 minutes west; course since yesterday noon north 78 degrees west 99 miles. I now considered myself nearly on a meridian with the east part of New Guinea.

Friday 22.
Strong gales from east-south-east to south-south-east, a high sea, and dark dismal night.

Our situation this day was extremely calamitous. We were obliged to take the course of the sea, running right before it and watching with the utmost care as the least error in the helm would in a moment have been our destruction.

At noon it blew very hard and the foam of the sea kept running over our stern and quarters; I however got propped up and made an observation of the latitude in 14 degrees 17 minutes south; course north 85 degrees west distance 130 miles; longitude made 29 degrees 38 minutes west.

The misery we suffered this night exceeded the preceding. The sea flew over us with great force and kept us baling with horror and anxiety.

Saturday 23.
At dawn of day I found everyone in a most distressed condition, and I began to fear that another such night would put an end to the lives of several

who seemed no longer able to support their sufferings. I served an allowance of two teaspoonfuls of
rum, after drinking which, having wrung our
clothes and taken our breakfast of bread and water,
we became a little refreshed.

Towards noon the weather became fair, but with
very little abatement of the gale and the sea remained
equally high. With some difficulty I observed the
latitude to be 13 degrees 44 minutes south: course
since yesterday noon north 74 degrees west, distance
116 miles; longitude made 31 degrees 32 minutes
west from Tofoa.

The wind moderated in the evening and the
weather looked much better, which rejoiced all
hands so that they ate their scanty allowance with
more satisfaction than for some time past. The night
also was fair but, being always wet with the sea, we
suffered much from the cold.

Sunday 24.

A fine morning, I had the pleasure to see, produced
some cheerful countenances and, the first time for 15
days past, we experienced comfort from the warmth
of the sun. We stripped and hung our clothes up to
dry, which were by this time become so threadbare
that they would not keep out either wet or cold.

At noon I observed in latitude 13 degrees 33
minutes south; longitude by account from Tofoa 33

degrees 28 minutes west; course north 84 degrees west, distance 114 miles. With the usual allowance of bread and water for dinner I served an ounce of pork to each person. This afternoon we had many birds about us which are never seen far from land, such as boobies and noddies.

Allowance Lessened.

As the sea began to run fair, and we shipped but little water, I took the opportunity to examine into the state of our bread and found that, according to the present mode of issuing, there was a sufficient quantity remaining for 29 days allowance, by which time I hoped we should be able to reach Timor. But as this was very uncertain and it was possible that, after all, we might be obliged to go to Java, I determined to proportion the allowance so as to make our stock hold out six weeks. I was apprehensive that this would be ill received, and that it would require my utmost resolution to enforce it for, small as the quantity was which I intended to take away for our future good, yet it might appear to my people like robbing them of life, and some, who were less patient than their companions, I expected would very ill brook it. However on my representing the necessity of guarding against delays that might be occasioned in our voyage by contrary winds, or other causes, and promising to enlarge upon the allowance as we got on, they cheerfully agreed to my proposal. It was accordingly settled that every person should receive one 25th of a pound of bread for breakfast, and the same quantity for dinner, so that by omitting the proportion for supper, we had 43 days allowance.

Monday 25.

At noon some noddies came so near to us that one of them was caught by hand. This bird was about the size of a small pigeon. I divided it with its entrails into 18 portions, and by a well-known method at sea of Who shall have this? it was distributed with the allowance of bread and water for dinner, and ate up bones and all, with salt water for sauce. I observed the latitude 13 degrees 32 minutes south; longitude made 35 degrees 19 minutes west; course north 89 degrees west, distance 108 miles.

In the evening, several boobies flying very near to us, we had the good fortune to catch one of them. This bird is as large as a duck: like the noddy it has received its name from seamen for suffering itself to be caught on the masts and yards of ships. They are the most presumptive proofs of being in the neighbourhood of land of any seafowl we are acquainted with. I directed the bird to be killed for supper, and the blood to be given to three of the people who were the most distressed for want of food. The body, with the entrails, beak, and feet, I divided into 18

shares, and with an allowance of bread, which I
made a merit of granting, we made a good supper,
compared with our usual fare.

Tuesday 26.

Fresh breezes from the south-east with fine weather.
In the morning we caught another booby so that
Providence appeared to be relieving our wants in an
extraordinary manner. Towards noon we passed a
great many pieces of the branches of trees, some of
which appeared to have been no long time in the
water. I had a good observation for the latitude, and
found our situation to be in 13 degrees 41 minutes
south; longitude by account from Tofoa 37 degrees
13 minutes west; course south 85 degrees west, 112
miles. The people were overjoyed at the addition to
their dinner which was distributed in the same manner as on the preceding evening, giving the blood to
those who were the most in want of food.

To make the bread a little savoury most of the
people frequently dipped it in salt water; but I generally broke mine into small pieces and ate it in my
allowance of water, out of a coconut shell with a
spoon, economically avoiding to take too large a
piece at a time, so that I was as long at dinner as if it
had been a much more plentiful meal.

The weather was now serene, which nevertheless
was not without its inconveniences, for we began to

feel distress of a different kind from that which we had lately been accustomed to suffer. The heat of the sun was so powerful that several of the people were seized with a languor and faintness which made life indifferent. We were so fortunate as to catch two boobies in the evening: their stomachs contained several flying-fish and small cuttlefish, all of which I saved to be divided for dinner the next day.

Wednesday 27.

A fresh breeze at east-south-east with fair weather. We passed much driftwood this forenoon and saw many birds; I therefore did not hesitate to pronounce that we were near the reefs of New Holland. From my recollection of Captain Cook's survey of this coast I considered the direction of it to be north-west, and I was therefore satisfied that, with the wind to the southward of east, I could always clear any dangers.

At noon I observed in latitude 13 degrees 26 minutes south; course since yesterday north 82 degrees west, distance 109 miles; longitude made 39 degrees 4 minutes. After writing my account I divided the two birds with their entrails and the contents of their maws into 18 portions and, as the prize was a very valuable one it was divided as before, by calling out Who shall have this? so that today, with the allowance of a 25th of a pound of bread at breakfast, and another at dinner, with the proportion of water, I was happy to see that every person thought he had feasted.

In the evening we saw a gannet; and the clouds remained so fixed in the west that I had little doubt of our being near the land. The people, after taking their allowance of water for supper, amused themselves with conversing on the probability of what we should find.

Thursday 28.

At one in the morning the person at the helm heard the sound of breakers, and I no sooner lifted up my head than I saw them close under our lee, not more than a quarter of a mile distant from us. I immediately hauled on a wind to the north-north-east and in ten minutes time we could neither see nor hear them.

I have already mentioned my reason for making New Holland so far to the southward: for I never doubted of numerous openings in the reef through which I could have access to the shore and, knowing the inclination of the coast to be to the north-west and the wind mostly to the southward of east, I could with ease range such a barrier of reefs till I should find a passage, which now became absolutely necessary, without a moment's loss of time. The idea of getting into smooth water and finding refreshments kept my people's spirits up: their joy was very great after we had got clear of the breakers to which we had approached much nearer than I thought was possible, without first discovering them.

Friday 29.

In the morning at daylight, we could see nothing of the land or of the reefs. We bore away again and at nine o'clock saw the reefs. The sea broke furiously over every part, and we had no sooner got near to them than the wind came at east, so that we could only lie along the line of the breakers, within which we saw the water so smooth that every person already anticipated the heart-felt satisfaction he should receive as soon as we could get within them. I now found we were embayed for we could not lie clear with the sails, the wind having backed against us; and the sea set in so heavy towards the reef that our situation had become unsafe. We could effect but little with the oars, having scarce strength to pull them, and I began to apprehend that we should be obliged to attempt pushing over the reef. Even this I did not despair of effecting with success when happily we discovered a break in the reef, about one mile from us, and at the same time an island of a moderate height within it, nearly in the same direction, bearing west half north. I entered the passage with a strong stream running to the westward and found it about a quarter of a mile broad, with every appearance of deep water.

On the outside the reef inclined to the north-east for a few miles, and from thence to the north-west: on the south side of the entrance it inclined to the south-south-west as far as I could see it, and I conjecture that a similar passage to this which we now entered may be found near the breakers that I first discovered which are 23 miles south of this channel.

I did not recollect what latitude Providential channel lies in, but I considered it to be within a few miles of this, which is situate in 12 degrees 51 minutes south latitude.

Being now happily within the reefs and in smooth water I endeavoured to keep near them to try for fish, but the tide set us to the north-west, I therefore bore away in that direction and, having promised to land on the first convenient spot we could find, all our past hardships seemed already to be forgotten.

At noon I had a good observation by which our latitude was 12 degrees 46 minutes south, whence the foregoing situations may be considered as determined with some exactness. The island first seen bore west-south-west five leagues. This, which I have called the island Direction, will in fair weather always show the channel, from which it bears due west, and may be seen as soon as the reefs from a ship's masthead: it lies in the latitude of 12 degrees 51 minutes south. These however are marks too small for a ship to hit unless it can hereafter be ascertained that passages through the reef are numerous along the coast which I am inclined to think they are, in which case there would be little risk even if the wind was directly on the shore.

My longitude made by dead reckoning from the island Tofoa to our passage through the reef is 40 degrees 10 minutes west. Providential channel, I imagine, must lie very nearly under the same meridian with our passage, by which it appears we had out-run our reckoning 1 degree 9 minutes.

We now returned God thanks for his gracious protection, and with much content took our miserable allowance of a 25th of a pound of bread and a quarter of a pint of water for dinner.

The Test

[HOMER]

When the child of morning, rosy-fingered Dawn, appeared, Ulysses put on his shirt and cloak, while the goddess wore a dress of a light gossamer fabric, very fine and graceful, with a beautiful golden girdle about her waist and a veil to cover her head. She at once set herself to think how she could speed Ulysses on his way. So she gave him a great bronze axe that suited his hands; it was sharpened on both sides, and had a beautiful olive-wood handle fitted firmly on to it. She also gave him a sharp adze, and then led the way to the far end of the island where the largest trees grew—alder, poplar and pine, that reached the sky— very dry and well seasoned, so as to sail light for him in the water. Then, when she had shown him where the best trees grew, Calypso went home, leaving him to cut them, which he soon finished doing. He cut down twenty trees in all and adzed them smooth, squaring them by rule in good workmanlike fashion.

Meanwhile Calypso came back with some augers, so he bored holes with them and fitted the timbers together with bolts and rivets. He made the raft as broad as a skilled shipwright makes the beam of a large vessel, and he fixed a deck on top of the ribs, and ran a gunwale all round it. He also made a mast with a yard arm, and a rudder to steer with. He fenced the raft all round with wicker hurdles as a protection against the waves, and then he threw on a quantity of wood. By and by Calypso brought him some linen to make the sails, and he made these too, excellently, making them fast with braces and sheets. Last of all, with the help of levers, he drew the raft down into the water.

In four days he had completed the whole work, and on the fifth Calypso sent him from the island after washing him and giving him some clean clothes. She gave him a goat skin full of black wine, and another larger one of water; she also gave him a wallet full of provisions, and found him in much good meat. Moreover, she made the wind fair and warm for him, and gladly did Ulysses spread his sail before it, while he sat and guided the raft skillfully by means of the rudder. He never closed his eyes, but kept them fixed on the Pleiads, on late-setting

Bootes, and on the Bear—which men also call the wain, and which turns round and round where it is, facing Orion, and alone never dipping into the stream of Oceanus—for Calypso had told him to keep this to his left. Days seven and ten did he sail over the sea, and on the eighteenth the dim outlines of the mountains on the nearest part of the Phaeacian coast appeared, rising like a shield on the horizon.

But King Neptune, who was returning from the Ethiopians, caught sight of Ulysses a long way off, from the mountains of the Solymi. He could see him sailing upon the sea, and it made him very angry, so he wagged his head and muttered to himself, saying, "Good heavens, so the gods have been changing their minds about Ulysses while I was away in Ethiopia, and now he is close to the land of the Phaeacians, where it is decreed that he shall escape from the calamities that have befallen him. Still, he shall have plenty of hardship yet before he has done with it."

Thereon he gathered his clouds together, grasped his trident, stirred it round in the sea, and roused the rage of every wind that blows till earth, sea, and sky were hidden in cloud, and night sprang forth out of the heavens. Winds from East, South, North, and West fell upon him all at the same time, and a tremendous sea got up, so that Ulysses' heart began to fail him. "Alas," he said to himself in his dismay, "what ever will become of me? I am afraid Calypso was right when she said I should have trouble by sea before I got back home. It is all coming true. How black is Jove making heaven with his clouds, and what a sea the winds are raising from every quarter at once. I am now safe to perish. Blest and thrice blest were those Danaans who fell before Troy in the cause of the sons of Atreus. Would that I had been killed on the day when the Trojans were pressing me so sorely about the dead body of Achilles, for then I should have had due burial and the Achaeans would have honoured my name; but now it seems that I shall come to a most pitiable end."

As he spoke a sea broke over him with such terrific fury that the raft reeled again, and he was carried overboard a long way off. He let go the helm, and the force of the hurricane was so great that it broke the mast half way up, and both sail and yard went over into the sea. For a long time Ulysses was under water, and it was all he could do to rise to the surface again, for the clothes Calypso had given him weighed him down; but at last he got his head above water and spat out the bitter brine that was running down his face in streams. In spite of all this, how-ever, he did not lose sight of his raft, but swam as fast as he could towards it, got hold of it, and climbed on board again so as to escape drowning. The sea took the raft and tossed it about as Autumn winds whirl thistledown round and round upon a road. It was as though the South, North, East, and West winds were all playing battledore and shuttlecock with it at once.

When he was in this plight, Ino daughter of Cadmus, also called Leucothea, saw him. She had formerly been a mere mortal, but had been since raised to the rank of a marine goddess. Seeing in what great distress Ulysses now was, she had compassion upon him, and, rising like a sea-gull from the waves, took her seat upon the raft.

"My poor good man," said she, "why is Neptune so furiously angry with you? He is giving you a great deal of trouble, but for all his bluster he will not kill you. You seem to be a sensible person, do then as I bid you; strip, leave your raft to drive before the wind, and swim to the Phaeacian coast where better luck awaits you. And here, take my veil and put it round your chest; it is enchanted, and you can come to no harm so long as you wear it. As soon as you touch land take it off, throw it back as far as you can into the sea, and then go away again." With these words she took off her veil and gave it him. Then she dived down again like a sea-gull and vanished beneath the dark blue waters.

But Ulysses did not know what to think. "Alas," he said to himself in his dismay, "this is only some one or other of the gods who is luring me to ruin by advising me to quit my raft. At any rate I will not do so at present, for the land where she said I should be quit of all troubles seemed to be still a good way off. I know what I will do—I am sure it will be best— no matter what happens I will stick to the raft as long as her timbers hold together, but when the sea breaks her up I will swim for it; I do not see how I can do any better than this."

While he was thus in two minds, Neptune sent a terrible great wave that seemed to rear itself above his head till it broke right over the raft, which then went to pieces as though it were a heap of dry chaff tossed about by a whirlwind. Ulysses got astride of one plank and rode upon it as if he were on horseback; he then took off the clothes Calypso had given him, bound Ino's veil under his arms, and plunged into the sea—meaning to swim on to shore. King Neptune watched him as he did so, and wagged his head, muttering to himself and saying, "There now, swim up and down as you best can till you fall in with well-to-do people. I do not think you will be able to say that I have let you off too lightly." On this he lashed his horses and drove to Aegae where his palace is.

But Minerva resolved to help Ulysses, so she bound the ways of all the winds except one, and made them lie quite still; but she roused a good stiff breeze from the North that should lay the waters till Ulysses reached the land of the Phaeacians where he would be safe.

Thereon he floated about for two nights and two days in the water, with a heavy swell on the sea and death staring him in the face; but when the third day broke, the wind fell and there was a dead calm without so much as a breath of air stirring. As he rose on the swell he looked eagerly ahead, and could see land quite near. Then, as children rejoice when their dear father begins to get better after having for a long time borne sore affliction sent him by some angry spirit, but the gods deliver him from evil, so was Ulysses thankful when he again saw land and trees, and swam on with all his strength that he might once more set foot upon dry ground. When, however, he got within earshot, he began to hear the surf thundering up against the rocks, for the swell still broke against them with a terrific roar. Everything was enveloped in spray; there were no harbours where a ship might ride, nor shelter of any kind, but only headlands, low-lying rocks, and mountain tops.

Ulysses' heart now began to fail him, and he said despairingly to himself, "Alas, Jove has let me see land after swimming so far that I had given up all hope, but I can find no landing place, for the coast is rocky and surf-beaten, the rocks are smooth and rise sheer from the sea, with deep water close under them so that I cannot climb out for want of foot hold. I am afraid some great wave will lift me off my legs and dash me against the rocks as I leave the water—which would give me a sorry landing. If, on the other hand, I swim further in search of some shelving beach or harbour, a hurricane may carry me out to sea again sorely against my will, or heaven may send some great monster of the deep to attack me; for Amphitrite breeds many such, and I know that Neptune is very angry with me."

While he was thus in two minds a wave caught him and took him with such force against the rocks that he would have been smashed and torn to pieces if Minerva had not shown him what to do. He caught hold of the rock with both hands and clung to it groaning with pain till the wave retired, so he was saved that time; but presently the wave came on again and carried him back with it far into the sea—tearing his hands as the suckers of a polypus are torn when some one plucks it from its bed, and the stones come up along with it—even so did the rocks tear the skin from his strong hands, and then the wave drew him deep down under the water.

Here poor Ulysses would have certainly perished even in spite of his own destiny, if Minerva had not helped him to keep his wits about him. He swam seaward again, beyond reach of the surf that was beating against the land, and at the same time he kept looking towards the shore to see if he could find some haven, or a spit that should take the waves aslant. By and by, as he swam on, he came to the mouth of a river, and here he thought would be the best place, for there were no rocks, and it afforded shelter from the wind. He felt that there was a current, so he prayed inwardly and said:

"Hear me, O King, whoever you may be, and save me from the anger of the sea-god Neptune, for I approach you prayerfully. Any one who has lost his way has at all times a claim even upon the gods, wherefore in my distress I draw near to your stream, and cling to the knees of your riverhood. Have mercy upon me, O king, for I declare myself your suppliant."

Then the god staid his stream and stilled the waves, making all calm before him, and bringing him safely into the mouth of the river. Here at last Ulysses' knees and strong hands failed him, for the sea had completely broken him. His body was all swollen, and his mouth and nostrils ran down like a river with seawater, so that he could neither breathe nor speak, and lay swooning from sheer exhaustion; presently, when he had got his breath and came to himself again, he took off the scarf that Ino had given him and threw it back into the salt stream of the river, whereon Ino received it into her hands from the wave that bore it towards her. Then he left the river, laid himself down among the rushes, and kissed the bounteous earth.

"Alas," he cried to himself in his dismay, "what ever will become of me, and how is it all to end? If I stay here upon the river bed through the long watches of the night, I am so exhausted that the bitter cold and damp may make an end of me—for towards sunrise there will be a keen wind blowing from off the river. If, on the other hand, I climb the hill side, find shelter in the woods, and sleep in some thicket, I may escape the cold and have a good night's rest, but some savage beast may take advantage of me and devour me."

In the end he deemed it best to take to the woods, and he found one upon some high ground not far from the water. There he crept beneath two shoots of olive that grew from a single stock—the one an ungrafted sucker, while the other had been grafted. No wind, however squally, could break through the cover they afforded, nor could the sun's rays pierce them, nor the rain get through them, so closely did they grow into one another. Ulysses crept under these and began to make himself a bed to lie on, for there was a great litter of dead leaves lying about—enough to make a covering for two or three men even in hard winter weather. He was glad enough to see this, so he laid himself down and heaped the leaves all round him. Then, as one who lives alone in the country, far from any neighbor, hides a brand as fire-seed in the ashes to save himself from having to get a light elsewhere, even so did Ulysses cover himself up with leaves; and Minerva shed a sweet sleep upon his eyes, closed his eyelids, and made him lose all memories of his sorrows.

A Draft in a Man-of-War

[HERMAN MELVILLE]

We were not many days out of port, when a rumour was set afloat that dreadfully alarmed many tars. It was this: that, owing to some unprecedented oversight in the Purser, or some equally unprecedented remissness in the Naval-storekeeper at Callao, the frigate's supply of that delectable beverage, called "grog," was well-nigh expended.

In the American Navy, the law allows one gill of spirits per day to every seaman. In two portions, it is served out just previous to breakfast and dinner. At the roll of the drum, the sailors assemble round a large tub, or cask, filled with liquid; and, as their names are called off by a midshipman, they step up and regale themselves from a little tin measure called a "tot." No high-liver helping himself to Tokay off a well-polished sideboard, smacks his lips with more mighty satisfaction than the sailor does over this *tot*. To many of them, indeed, the thought of their daily *tots* forms a perpetual perspective of ravishing landscapes, indefinitely receding in the distance.

It is their great "prospect in life." Take away their grog, and life possesses no further charms for them. It is hardly to be doubted, that the controlling inducement which keeps many men in the Navy, is the unbounded confidence they have in the ability of the United States government to supply them, regularly and unfailingly, with their daily allowance of this beverage. I have known several forlorn individuals, shipping as landsmen, who have confessed to me, that having contracted a love for ardent spirits, which they could not renounce, and having by their foolish courses been brought into the most abject poverty—insomuch that they could no longer gratify their thirst ashore—they incontinently entered the Navy; regarding it as the asylum for all drunkards, who might there prolong their lives by regular hours and exercise, and twice every day quench their thirst by moderate and undeviating doses.

When I once remonstrated with an old toper of a top-man about this daily dram-drinking; when I told him it was ruining him, and advised him to *stop his grog* and receive the money for it, in addition to his wages as provided by law, he turned about on me, with an irresistibly waggish look, and said, "Give up my grog? And why? Because it is ruining me? No, no; I am a good Christian, White-Jacket, and love my enemy too much to drop his acquaintance."

It may be readily imagined, therefore, what consternation and dismay pervaded the gun-deck at the first announcement of the tidings that the grog was expended.

"The grog gone!" roared an old Sheet-anchor-man.

"Oh! Lord! what a pain in my stomach!" cried a Main-top-man.

"It's worse than the cholera!" cried a man of the After-guard.

"I'd sooner the water-casks would give out!" said a Captain of the Hold.

"Are we ganders and geese, that we can live without grog?" asked a Corporal of Marines.

"Ay, we must now drink with the ducks!" cried a Quarter-master.

"Not a tot left?" groaned a Waister.

"Not a toothful!" sighed a Holder, from the bottom of his boots.

Yes, the fatal intelligence proved true. The drum was no longer heard rolling the men to the tub, and deep gloom and dejection fell like a cloud. The ship was like a great city, when some terrible calamity has overtaken it. The men stood apart, in groups, discussing their woes, and mutually condoling. No longer, of still moonlight nights, was the song heard from the giddy tops; and few and far between were the stories that were told. It was during this interval, so dismal to many, that to the amazement of all hands, ten men were reported by the master-at-arms to be intoxicated. They were brought up to the mast, and at their appearance the doubts of the most skeptical were dissipated; but whence they had obtained their liquor no one could tell. It was observed, however at the time, that the tarry knaves all smelled of lavender, like so many dandies.

After their examination they were ordered into the "brig," a jail-house between two guns on the main-deck, where prisoners are kept. Here they laid for some time, stretched out stark and stiff, with their arms folded over their breasts, like so many effigies of the Black Prince on his monument in Canterbury Cathedral.

Their first slumbers over, the marine sentry who stood guard over them had as much as he could do to keep off the crowd, who were all eagerness to find out how, in such a time of want, the prisoners had managed to drink themselves into oblivion. In due time they were liberated, and the secret simultaneously leaked out.

It seemed that an enterprising man of their number, who had suffered severely from the common deprivation, had all at once been struck by a brilliant idea. It had come to his knowledge that the purser's steward was supplied with a large quantity of *Eau-de-Cologne*, clandestinely brought out in the ship, for the purpose of selling it on his own account, to the people of the coast; but the supply proving larger than the demand, and having no customers on board the frigate but Lieutenant Selvagee, he was now carrying home more than a third of his original stock. To make a short story of it, this functionary, being called upon in secret, was readily prevailed upon to part with a dozen bottles, with whose contents the intoxicated party had regaled themselves.

The news spread far and wide among the men, being only kept secret from the officers and underlings, and that night the long, crane-necked Cologne bottles jingled in out-of-the-way corners and by-places, and, being emptied, were sent flying out of the ports. With brown sugar, taken from the mess-chests, and hot water begged from the galley-cooks, the men made all manner of punches, toddies, and cocktails, letting fall therein a small drop of tar, like a bit of brown toast, by way of imparting a flavour. Of course, the thing was managed with the utmost secrecy; and as a whole dark night elapsed after their orgies, the revellers were, in a good measure, secure from detection; and those who indulged too freely had twelve long hours to get sober before daylight obtruded.

Next day, fore and aft, the whole frigate smelled like a lady's toilet; the very tar-buckets were fragrant; and from the mouth of many a grim, grizzled old quarter-gunner came the most fragrant of breaths. The amazed Lieutenants went about snuffing up the gale; and, for once, Selvagee had no further need to flourish his perfumed hand-kerchief. It was as if we were sailing by some odoriferous shore, in the vernal season of violets. Sabaean odours!

> "For many a league,
> Cheered with grateful smell, old Ocean smiled."

But, alas! all this perfume could not be wasted for nothing; and the masters-at-arms and ship's corporals, putting this and that together, very soon burrowed into the secret. The purser's steward was called to account, and no more lavender punches and Cologne toddies were drank on board the *Neversink*.

An Unknown Species
of Whale

[JULES VERNE]

The year 1866 was signalized by a remarkable incident, a mysterious and inexplicable phenomenon, which doubtless no one has yet forgotten. Not to mention rumors which agitated the maritime population, and excited the public mind, even in the interior of continents, seafaring men were particularly excited. Merchants, common sailors, captains of vessels, skippers, both of Europe and America, naval officers of all countries, and the governments of several states on the two continents, were deeply interested in the matter.

For some time past, vessels had been met by "an enormous thing," a long object, spindle-shaped, occasionally phosphorescent, and infinitely larger and more rapid in its movements than a whale.

The facts relating to this apparition (entered in various log-books) agreed in most respects as to the shape of the object or creature in question, the untiring rapidity of its movements, its surprising power of locomotion, and the peculiar life with which it seemed endowed. If it was a cetacean, it surpassed in size all those hitherto classified in science. Taking into consideration the mean of observations made at divers times—rejecting the timid estimate of those who assigned to this object a length of two hundred feet, equally with the exaggerated opinions which set it down as a mile in width and three in length— we might fairly conclude that this mysterious being surpassed greatly all dimensions admitted by the ichthyologists of the day, if it existed at all. And that it did exist was an undeniable fact; and, with that tendency which disposes the human mind in favor of the marvelous, we can understand the excitement produced in the entire world by the supernatural apparition. As to classing it in the list of fables, the idea was out of the question.

Captain Farragut was a good seaman, worthy of the frigate he commanded. His vessel and he were one. He was the soul of it. On the question of the cetacean there was no doubt in his mind, and he would not allow the existence of the animal to be disputed on board. He believed in it as certain good women believe in the leviathan—by faith, not by reason. The monster did exist, and he had sworn to rid the seas of it. He was a kind of Knight of Rhodes, a second Dieudonné de Gozon, going to meet the serpent which desolated the island. Either Captain Farragut would kill the narwhal, or the narwhal would kill the captain. There was no third course.

The officers on board shared the opinion of their chief. They were ever chatting, discussing, and calculating the various chances of a meeting, watching narrowly the vast surface of the ocean. More than one took up his quarters voluntarily in the cross-trees, who would have cursed such a berth under any other circumstances. As long as the sun described its daily course, the rigging was crowded with sailors, whose feet were burned to such an extent by the heat of the deck as to render it unbearable; still the *Abraham Lincoln* had not yet breasted the suspected waters of the Pacific. As to the ship's company, they desired nothing better than to meet the unicorn, to harpoon it, hoist it on board, and dispatch it. They watched the sea with eager attention.

Besides, Captain Farragut had spoken of a certain sum of two thousand dollars, set apart for whoever should first sight the monster, were he cabin-boy, common seaman, or officer.

I leave you to judge how eyes were used on board the *Abraham Lincoln*.

The 20th of July, the tropic of Capricorn was cut by 105° of longitude, and the 27th of the same month we crossed the equator on the 110th meridian. This passed, the frigate took a more decided westerly direction, and scoured the central waters of the Pacific. Commander Farragut thought, and with reason, that it was better to remain in deep water, and keep clear of continents or islands, which the beast itself seemed to shun (perhaps because there was not enough water for him! suggested the greater part of the crew). The frigate passed at some distance from the Marquesas and the Sandwich Islands, crossed the tropic of Cancer, and made for the China Seas. We were on the theater of the last diversions of the monster; and to say truth, we no longer *lived* on board. Heats palpitated, fearfully preparing themselves for future incurable aneurism. The entire ship's crew were undergoing a nervous excitement, of which I can give no idea; they could not eat, they could not sleep: twenty times a day, a misconception or an optical illusion of some sailor seated on the taffrail would cause dreadful perspirations, and these emotions, twenty times repeated, kept us in a state of excitement so violent that a reaction was unavoidable.

And truly, reaction soon showed itself. For three months, during which a day seemed an age, the *Abraham Lincoln* furrowed all the waters of the Northern Pacific, running at whales, making sharp deviations from her course, veering suddenly from one tack to another, stopping suddenly, putting on steam, and backing ever and anon at the risk of deranging her machinery; and not one point of the Japanese or American coast was left unexplored.

The warmest partisans of the enterprise now became its most ardent detractors. Reaction mounted from the crew to the captain himself, and certainly, had it not been for resolute determination on the part of Captain Farragut, the frigate would have headed due southward. This useless search could not last much longer. The *Abraham Lincoln* had nothing to reproach herself with, she had done her best to succeed. Never had an American ship's crew shown more zeal or patience; its failure could not be placed to their charge—there remained nothing but to return.

This was represented to the commander. The sailors could not hide their discontent, and the service suffered. I will not say there was a mutiny on board, but after a reasonable period of obstinacy, Captain Farragut (as Columbus did) asked for three days' patience. If in three days the monster did not appear, the man at the helm should give three turns of the wheel, and the *Abraham Lincoln* would make for the European seas.

This promise was made on the 2nd of November. It had the effect of rallying the ship's crew. The ocean was watched with renewed attention. Each one wished for a last glance in which to sum up his remembrance. Glasses were used with feverish activity. It was a grand defiance given to the giant narwhal, and he could scarcely fail to answer the summons and "appear."

Two days passed, the steam was at half-pressure; a thousand schemes were tried to attract the attention and stimulate the apathy of the animal in case it should be met in those parts. Large quantities of bacon were trailed in the wake of the ship, to the great satisfaction (I must say) of the sharks. Small craft radiated in all directions round the *Abraham Lincoln* as she lay to, and did not leave a spot of the sea unexplored. But the night of the 4th of November arrived without the unveiling of this submarine mystery.

The next day, the 5th of November, at twelve, the delay would (morally speaking) expire; after that time, Commander Farragut, faithful to his promise, was to turn the course to the southeast and abandon forever the northern regions of the Pacific.

The frigate was then in 31° 15′ north latitude and 136° 42′ east longitude. The coast of Japan still remained less than two hundred miles to leeward. Night was approaching. They had just struck eight bells; large clouds veiled the face of the moon, then in its first quarter. The sea undulated peaceably under the stern of the vessel.

At that moment I was leaning forward on the starboard netting. Conseil, standing near me, was looking straight before him. The crew, perched in the ratlines, examined the horizon, which contracted and darkened by degrees. Officers with their nightglasses scoured the growing darkness; sometimes the ocean sparkled under the rays of the moon, which darted between two clouds, then all trace of light was lost in the darkness.

In looking at Conseil, I could see he was undergoing a little of the general influence. At least I thought so. Perhaps for the first time his nerves vibrated to a sentiment of curiosity.

"Come, Conseil," said I, "this is the last chance of pocketing the two thousand dollars."

"May I be permitted to say, sir," replied Conseil, "that I never reckoned on getting the prize; and, had the government of the Union offered a hundred thousand dollars, it would have been one the poorer."

"You are right, Conseil. It is a foolish affair after all, and one upon which we entered too lightly. What time lost, what useless emotions! We should have been back in France six months ago."

"In your little room, sir," replied Conseil, "and in your museum, sir; and I should have already classed all your fossils, sir. And the Babiroussa would have been installed in its cage in the Jardin des Plantes, and have drawn al the curious people of the capital!"

"As you say, Conseil. I fancy we shall run a fair chance of being laughed at for our pains."

"That's tolerably certain," replied Conseil quietly; "I think they will make fun of you, sir. And—must I say it?—"

"Go on, my good friend."

"Well, sir, you will only get your deserts."

"Indeed!"

"When one has the honor of being a savant as you are, sire, one should not expose one's self to—"

Conseil had not time to finish his compliment. In the midst of general silence a voice had just been heard. It was the voice of Ned Land shouting.

"Look out there! The very thing we are looking for—on our weather beam!"

At this cry the whole ship's crew hurried toward the harpooner—commander, officers, masters, sailors, cabin-boys; even the engineers left their engines, and the stokers their furnaces.

The order to stop her had been given, and the frigate now simply went on by her own momentum. The darkness was then profound; and however good the Canadian's eyes were, I asked myself how he had managed to see, and what he has been able to see. My heart beat as if it would break. But Ned Land was not mistaken, and we all perceived the object he pointed to. At two cables' lengths from the *Abraham Lincoln*, on the starboard quarter, the sea seemed to be illuminated all over. It was not a mere phosphoric phenomenon. The monster emerged some fathoms from the water, and then threw out that very intense but inexplicable light mentioned in the report of several captains. This magnificent irradiation must have been produced by an agent of great *shining* power. The luminous part traced on the sea an immense oval, most elongated, the center of which condensed a burning heat, whose overpowering brilliancy died out by successive gradations.

"It is only an agglomeration of phosphoric particles," cried one of the officers.

"No, sir, certainly not," I replied. "Never did pholades of salpæ produce such a powerful light. That brightness is on an essentially electrical nature. Besides, see, see! It moves, it is moving forward, backward, it is darting toward us!"

A general cry arose from the frigate.

"Silence!" said the captain; "up with the helm, reverse the engines."

The steam was shut off, and the *Abraham Lincoln*, beating to port, described a semicircle.

"Right the helm, go ahead," cried the captain.

These orders were executed, and the frigate moved rapidly from the burning light.

I was mistaken. She tried to sheer off, but the supernatural animal approached with a velocity double her own.

We gasped for breath. Stupefaction more than fear made us dumb and motionless. The animal gained on us, sporting with the waves. It made the round of the frigate, which was then making four-teen knots, and enveloped it with its electric rings like luminous dust. Then it moved away two or three miles, leaving a phosphorescent track, like those volumes of steam that the express trains leave behind. All at once from the dark line of the hori-zon whither it retired to gain its momentum, the monster rushed suddenly toward the *Abraham Lin-coln* with alarming rapidity, stopped suddenly about twenty feet from the hull, and died out—not diving under the water, for its brilliancy did not abate—but suddenly, as if the source of this brilliant emanation was exhausted. Then it reappeared on the other side of the vessel, as if it had turned and slid under the hull. Any moment a collision might have occurred which would have been fatal to us. However, I was astonished at the maneuvers of the frigate. She fled and did not attack.

On the captain's face, generally so impassive, was an expression of unaccountable astonishment.

"Mr. Aronnax," he said, "I do not know with what formidable being I have to deal, and I will not prudently risk my frigate in the midst of this dark-ness. Besides, how attack this unknown thing, how defend one's self from it? Wait for daylight, and the scene will change."

"You have not further doubt, captain, of the nature of the animal?"

"No, sir; it is evidently a gigantic narwhal, and an electric one."

"Perhaps," added I, "one can only approach it with a gymnotus or a torpedo."

"Undoubtedly," replied the captain, "if it possesses such dreadful power, it is the most terrible animal that ever was created. That is why, sir, I must be on my guard."

The crew were on their feet all night. No one thought of sleep. The *Abraham Lincoln*, not being able to struggle with such velocity, had moderated its pace, and sailed at half speed. For its part, the narwhal, imitating the frigate, let the waves rock it at will, and seemed decided not to leave the scene of the struggle. Toward midnight, however, it disappeared, or, to use a more appropriate term, it "died out" like a large glowworm. Had it fled? One could only fear, not hope it. But at seven minutes to one o'clock in the morning a deafening whistling was heard, like that produced by a body of water rushing with great violence.

The captain, Ned Land, and I were then on the poop, eagerly peering through the profound darkness.

"Ned Land," asked the commander, "you have often heard the roaring of whales?"

"Often, sir; but never such whales the sight of which brought me in two thousand dollars. If I can only approach within four harpoon lengths of it!"

"But to approach it," said the commander, "I ought to put a whaler at your disposal?"

"Certainly, sir."

"That will be trifling with the lives of my men."

"And mine too," simply said the harpooner.

Toward two o'clock in the morning, the burning light reappeared, not less intense, about five miles to windward of the *Abraham Lincoln*. Notwithstanding the distance, and the noise of the wind and sea, one heard distinctly the loud strokes of the animal's tail, and even its painting breath. It seemed that, at the moment that the enormous narwhal had come to take breath at the surface of the water, the air was ingulfed in its lungs, like the steam in the vast cylinders of a machine of two thousand horsepower.

"Hum!" thought I, "a whale with the strength of a cavalry regiment would be a pretty whale!"

We were on the *qui vive* till daylight, and prepared for combat. The fishing implements were laid along the hammock nettings. The second lieutenant loaded the blunderbusses, which could throw harpoons to the distance of a mile, and long duck-guns, with explosive bullets, which inflicted mortal wounds even to the most terrible animals. Ned Land contented himself with sharpening his harpoon—a terrible weapon in his hands.

At six o'clock, day began to break; and with the first glimmer of light, the electric light of the narwhal disappeared. At seven o'clock the day was sufficiently advanced, but a very thick sea-fog obscured our view, and the best spy-glasses could not pierce it. That caused disappointment and anger.

I climbed the mizzen-mast. Some officers were already perched on the mast-heads. At eight o'clock the fog lay heavily on the waves, and its thick scrolls rose little by little. The horizon grew wider and clearer at the same time. Suddenly, just as on the day before, Ned Land's voice was heard.

"The thing itself on the port quarter!" cried the harpooner.

Every eye was turned toward the point indicated. There, a mile and a half from the frigate, a long blackish body emerged a yard above the waves. Its tail, violently agitated, produced a considerable eddy. Never did a caudal appendage beat the sea with such violence. An immense track, of a dazzling whiteness, marked the passage of the animal, and described a long curve.

The frigate approached the cetacean. I examined it thoroughly.

The reports of the Shannon and of the Helvetia had rather exaggerated its size, and I estimated its length at only two hundred and fifty feet. As to its dimensions, I could only conjecture them to be admirably proportioned. While I watched this phenomenon, two jets of steam and water were ejected from its vents, and rose to the height of 120 feet; thus I ascertained its way of breathing. I concluded definitely that it belonged to the vertebrate branch, class mammalia.

The crew waited impatiently for their chief's orders. The latter, after having observed the animal attentively, called the engineer. The engineer ran to him.

"Sir," said the commander, "you have steam up?"

"Yes, sir," answered the engineer.

"Well, make up your fires and put on all steam."

Three hurrahs greeted this order. The time for the struggle had arrived. Some moments after, the two funnels of the frigate vomited torrents of black smoke, and the bridge quaked under the trembling of the boilers.

The *Abraham Lincoln*, propelled by her powerful screw, went straight at the animal. The latter allowed it to come within half a cable's length; then, as if disdaining to dive, it took a little turn, and stopped a short distance off.

This pursuit lasted nearly three-quarters of an hour, without the frigate gaining two yards on the cetacean. It was quite evident that at that rate we should never come up with it.

"Well, Mr. Land," asked the captain, "do you advise me to put the boats out to sea?"

"No, sir," replied Ned Land; "because we shall not take that beast easily."

"What shall we do then?"

"Put on more steam if you can, sir. With your leave, I mean to post myself under the bowsprit, and if we get within harpooning distance, I shall throw my harpoon."

"Go, Ned," said the captain. "Engineer, put on more pressure."

Ned Land went to his post. The fires were increased, the screw revolved forty-three times a minute, and the steam poured out of the valves. We heaved the log, and calculated that the *Abraham Lincoln* was going at the rate of 18½ miles an hour.

But the accursed animal swam too at the rate of 18½ miles.

For a whole hour, the frigate kept up this pace, without gaining six feet. It was humiliating for one of the swiftest sailers in the American navy. A stubborn anger seized the crew; the sailors abused the monster, who, as before, disdained to answer them; the captain no longer contented himself with twisting his beard—he gnawed it.

The engineer was again called.

"You have turned full steam on?"

"Yes, sir," replied the engineer.

The speed of the *Abraham Lincoln* increased. Its masts trembled down to their stepping-holes, and the clouds of smoke could hardly find way out of the narrow funnels.

They heaved the log a second time.

"Well?" asked the captain of the man at the wheel.

"Nineteen miles and three-tenths, sir."

"Clap on more steam."

The engineer obeyed. The manometer showed ten degrees. But the cetacean grew warm itself, no doubt; for, without straining itself, it made $19\frac{3}{10}$ miles.

What a pursuit! No, I cannot describe the emotion that vibrated through me. Ned Land kept his post, harpoon in hand. Several times the animal let us gain upon it. "We shall catch it! We shall catch it!" cried the Canadian. But just as he was going to strike, the cetacean stole away with a rapidity that could not be estimated at less than thirty miles an hour, and even during our maximum of speed it bullied the frigate, going round and round it. A cry of fury broke from every one.

At noon we were no further advanced than at eight o'clock in the morning.

The captain then decided to take more direct means.

"Ah!" said he, "that animal goes quicker than the *Abraham Lincoln*. Very well! We will see whether it will escape these conical bullets. Send your men to the forecastle, sir."

The forecastle gun was immediately loaded and slewed round. But the shot passed some feet above the cetacean, which was half a mile off.

"Another more to the right," cried the commander, "and five dollars to whoever will hit that infernal beast."

An old gunner with a gray beard—that I can see now—with steady eye and grave face, went up to the gun and took a long aim. A loud report was heard, with which were mingled the cheers of the crew.

The bullet did its work; it hit the animal, but not fatally, and, sliding off the rounded surface, was lost in two miles' depth of sea.

The chase began again, and the captain, leaning toward me, said:

"I will pursue that beast till my frigate bursts up."

"Yes," answered I; "and you will be quite right to do it."

I wished the beast would exhaust itself, and not be insensible to fatigue, like a steam-engine! But it was of no use. Hours passed, without its showing any signs of exhaustion.

However, it must be said in praise of the *Abraham Lincoln*, that she struggled on indefatigably. I cannot reckon the distance she made under three hundred miles during this unlucky day, November the 6th. But night came on, and overshadowed the rough ocean.

Now I thought our expedition was at an end, and that we should never again see the extraordinary animal. I was mistaken. At ten minutes to eleven in the evening, the electric light reappeared three miles to windward of the frigate, as pure, as intense as during the preceding night.

The narwhal seemed motionless; perhaps, tired with its day's work, it slept, letting itself float with the undulation of the waves. Now was a chance of which the captain resolved to take advantage.

He gave his orders. The *Abraham Lincoln* kept up half-steam, and advanced cautiously so as not to awake its adversary. It is no rare thing to meet in the middle of the ocean whales so sound asleep that they can be successfully attacked, and Ned Land had harpooned more than one during its sleep. The Canadian went to take his place again under the bowsprit.

The frigate approached noiselessly, stopped at two cables' length from the animal, and following its track. No one breathed; a deep silence reigned on the bridge. We were not a hundred feet from the burning focus, the light of which increased and dazzled our eyes.

At this moment, leaning on the forecastle bulwark, I saw below me Ned Land grappling the martingale in one hand, brandishing his terrible harpoon in the other, scarcely twenty feet from the motionless animal. Suddenly his arm straightened, and the harpoon was thrown; I heard the sonorous stroke of the weapon, which seemed to have struck a hard body. The electric light went out suddenly, and two enormous waterspouts broke over the bridge of the frigate, rushing like a torrent from stem to stern, overthrowing men, and breaking the lashing of the spars. A fearful shock followed, and, thrown over the rail without having time to stop myself, I fell into the sea.

This unexpected fall so stunned me that I have no clear recollection of my sensations at the time. I was at first drawn down to a depth of about twenty feet. I am a good swimmer (though without pretending to rival Byron or Edgar Poe, who were masters of the art), and in that plunge I did not lose my presence of mind. Two vigorous strokes brought me to the surface of the water. My first care was to look for the frigate. Had the crew seen me disappear? Had the *Abraham Lincoln* veered round? Would the captain put out a boat? Might I hope to be saved?

The darkness was intense. I caught a glimpse of a black mass disappearing in the east, its beacon-lights dying out in the distance. It was the frigate! I was lost.

"Help! help!" I shouted, swimming toward the *Abraham Lincoln* in desperation.

My clothes encumbered me; they seemed glued to my body, and paralyzed my movements.

I was sinking! I was suffocating!

"Help!"

This was my last cry. My mouth filled with water; I struggled against being drawn down the abyss. Suddenly my clothes were seized by a strong hand, and I felt myself quickly drawn up to the surface of the sea; and I heard, yes, I heard these words pronounced in my ear:

"If master would be so good as to lean on my shoulder, master would swim with much greater ease."

I seized with one hand my faithful Conseil's arm.

"Is it you?" said I, "you?"

"Myself," answered Conseil; "and waiting master's orders."

"That shock threw you as well as me into the sea?"

"No, but being in my master's service, I followed him."

The worthy fellow thought that was but natural.

"And the frigate?" I asked.

"The frigate?" replied Conseil, turning on his back; "I think that master had better not count too much on her."

"You think so?"

"I say that, at the time I threw myself into the sea, I heard the men at the wheel say, 'The screw and the rudder are broken.'"

"Broken?"

"Yes, broken by the monster's teeth. It is the only injury the *Abraham Lincoln* has sustained. But it is a bad lookout for us—she no longer answers her helm."

"Then we are lost!"

"Perhaps so," calmly answered Conseil. "However, we have still several hours before us, and one can do a good deal in some hours."

Conseil's imperturbable coolness set me up again. I swam more vigorously; but, cramped by my clothes, which stuck to me like a leaden weight, I felt great difficulty in bearing up. Conseil saw this.

"Will master let me make a slit?" said he; and slipping an open knife under my clothes, he ripped them up from top to bottom very rapidly. Then he cleverly slipped them off me, while I swam for both of us.

Then I did the same for Conseil, and we continued to swim near to each other.

Nevertheless, out situation was no less terrible. Perhaps our disappearance had not been noticed; and if it had been, the frigate could not tack, being without its helm. Conseil argued on this supposition, and laid his plans accordingly. This phlegmatic boy was perfectly self-possessed. We then decided that, as our only chance of safety was being picked up by the *Abraham Lincoln*'s boats, we ought to manage so as to wait for them as long as possible. I resolved then to husband our strength, so that both should not be exhausted at the same time; and this is how we managed: while one of us lay on our back, quite still, with arms crossed, and legs stretched out, the other would swim and push the other on in front. This towing business did not last more than ten minutes each; and relieving each other thus, we could swim on for some hours, perhaps till daybreak. Poor chance! But hope is so firmly rooted in the heart of man! Moreover, there were two of us. Indeed, I declare (though it may seem improbable) if I sought to destroy all hope, if I wished to despair, I could not.

The collision of the frigate with the cetacean had occurred about eleven o'clock the evening before. I reckoned then we should have eight hours to swim before sunrise—an operation quite practicable if we relieved each other. The sea, very calm, was in our favor. Sometimes I tried to pierce the intense darkness that was only dispelled by the phosphorescence caused by our movements. I watched the luminous waves that broke over my hand, whose mirror-like surface was spotted with silvery rings. One might have said that we were in a bath of quicksilver.

Near one o'clock in the morning, I was seized with dreadful fatigue. My limbs stiffened under the strain of violent cramp. Conseil was obliged to keep me up, and our preservation devolved on him alone. I heard the poor boy pant; his breathing became short and hurried. I found that he could not keep up much longer.

"Leave me! Leave me!" I said to him.

"Leave my master? Never!" replied he. "I would drown first."

Just then the moon appeared through the fringes of a thick cloud that the wind was driving to the east. The surface of the sea glittered with its rays. This kindly light reanimated us. My head got better again. I looked at all the points of the horizon. I saw the frigate! She was five miles from us, and looked like a dark mass, hardly discernible. But no boats!

I would have cried out. But what good would it have been at such a distance? My swollen lips could utter no sounds. Conseil could articulate some words, and I heard him repeat at intervals, "Help! help!"

Our movements were suspended for an instant; we listened. It might be only a singing in the ear, but it seemed to me as if a cry answered the cry from Conseil.

"Did you hear?" I murmured.

"Yes! yes!"

And Conseil gave one more despairing call.

This time there was no mistake! A human voice responded to ours! Was it the voice of another unfortunate creature, abandoned in the middle of the ocean, some other victim of the shock sustained by the vessel? Or rather was it a boat from the frigate, that was hailing us in the darkness?

Conseil made last effort, and leaning on my shoulder, while I struck out in a despairing effort, he raised himself half out of the water, then fell back exhausted.

"What did you see?"

"I saw," murmured he—"I saw—but do not talk—reserve all your strength!"

What had he seen? Then, I know not why, the thought of the monster came into my head for the first time! But that voice? The time is past for Jonahs to take refuge in whales' bellies! However, Conseil was towing me again. He raised his head sometimes, looked before us, and uttered a cry of recognition, which was responded to by a voice that came nearer and nearer. I scarcely heard it. My strength was exhausted; my fingers stiffened; my hand afforded me support no longer; my mouth, convulsively opening, filled with salt water. Cold crept over me. I raised my head for the last time, then I sank.

At this moment a hard body struck me. I clung to it then I felt that I was being drawn up, that I was brought to the surface of the water, that my chest collapsed: I fainted.

It is certain that I soon came to, thanks to the vigorous rubbings that I received. I half opened my eyes.

"Conseil!" I murmured.

"Does master call me?" asked Conseil.

Just then, by the waning light of the moon, which was sinking down to the horizon, I saw a face which was not Conseil's, and which I immediately recognized.

"Ned!" I cried.

"The same, sir, who is seeking his prize!" replied the Canadian.

"Were you thrown into the sea by the shock of the frigate?"

"Yes, professor; but, more fortunate than you, I was able to find a footing almost directly upon a floating island."

"An island?"

"Or, more correctly speaking, on our gigantic narwhal."

"Explain yourself, Ned!"

"Only I soon found out why my harpoon had not entered its skin and was blunted."

"Why, Ned, why?"

"Because, professor, that beast is made of sheet-iron."

The Canadian's last words produced a sudden revolution in my brain. I wriggled myself quickly to the top of the being, or object, half out of the water, which served us for a refuge. I kicked it. It was evidently a hard, impenetrable body, and not the soft substance that forms the bodies of the great marine mammalia. But this hard body might be a bony cara-pace, like that of the antediluvian animals; and I should be free to class this monster among amphibi-ous reptiles, such as tortoises or alligators.

Well, no! The blackish back that supported me was smooth, polished, without scales. The blow produced a metallic sound; and incredible though it may be, it seemed, I might say, as if it was made of riveted plates.

There was no doubt about it! This monster, this natural phenomenon that had puzzled the learned world, and overthrown and misled the imagination of seamen of both hemispheres, was, it must be owned, a still more astonishing phenomenon, inas-much as it was a simply human construction.

We had no time to lose, however. We were lying upon the back of a sort of submarine boat, which appeared (as far as I could judge) like a huge fish of steel. Ned Land's mind was made up on this point. Conseil and I could only agree with him.

Just then a bubbling began at the back of this strange thing (which was evidently propelled by a screw), and it began to move. We had only just time to seize hold of the upper part, which rose about seven feet out of the water, and happily its speed was not great.

"As long as it sails horizontally," muttered Ned Land, "I do not mind; but it if takes a fancy to dive, I would not give two straws for my life."

The Canadian might have said still less. It became really necessary to communicate with the beings, whatever they were, shut up inside the machine. I searched all over the outside for an aperture, a panel, or a man-hole, to use a technical expression; but the lines of the iron rivets, solidly driven into the joints of the iron plates, were clear and uniform. Besides, the moon disappeared then, and left us in total darkness.

At last this long night passed. My indistinct remembrance prevents my describing all the impressions it made. I can only recall one circumstance. During some lulls of the wind and sea, I fancied I heard several times vague sounds, a sort of fugitive harmony produced by distant words of command. What was then the mystery of this submarine craft of which the whole world vainly sought an explanation? What kind of beings existed in this strange boat? What mechanical agent caused its prodigious speed?

Daybreak appeared. The morning mists surrounded us, but they soon cleared off. I was about to examine the hull, which formed on deck a kind of horizontal platform, when I felt it gradually sinking.

"Oh, confound it!' cried Ned Land, kicking the resounding plate; "open, you inhospitable rascals!"

Happily the sinking movement ceased. Suddenly a noise, like iron works violently pushed aside, came from the interior of the boat. One iron plate was moved, a man appeared, uttered an odd cry, and disappeared immediately.

Some moments after, eight strong men with masked faces appeared noiselessly, and drew us down into their formidable machine.

A Fatal Mistake

[HERMAN MELVILLE]

After the mysterious interview in the fore-chains—the one so abruptly ended there by Billy—nothing especially germane to the story occurred until the events now about to be narrated.

Elsewhere it has been said that in the lack of frigates (of course better sailers than line-of-battle ships) in the English squadron up the Straits at that period, the *Indomitable* was occasionally employed not only as an available substitute for a scout, but at times on detached service of more important kind. This was not alone because of her sailing qualities, not common in a ship of her rate, but quite as much, probably, that the character of her commander, it was thought, specially adapted him for any duty where under unforeseen difficulties a prompt initiative might have to be taken in some matter demanding knowledge and ability in addition to those qualities implied in good seamanship. It was on an expedition of the latter sort, a somewhat distant one, and when the Indomitable was almost at her furthest remove from the fleet, that in the latter part of an afternoon-watch she unexpectedly came in sight of a ship of the enemy. It proved to be a frigate. The latter perceiving thro' the glass that the weight of men and metal would be heavily against her, invoking her light heels, crowded sail to get away. After a chase urged almost against hope and lasting until about the middle of the first dog-watch, she signally succeeded in effecting her escape.

Not long after the pursuit had been given up, and ere the excitement incident thereto had altogether waned away, the Master-at-arms, ascending from his cavernous sphere, made his appearance cap in hand by the main-mast, respectfully waiting the notice of Captain Vere then solitary walking the weather-side of the quarterdeck, doubtless somewhat chafed at the failure of the pursuit. The spot where Claggart stood was the place allotted to men of lesser grades seeking some more particular interview either with the officer-of-the-deck or the Captain himself. But from the latter it was not often that a sailor or petty-officer of those days would seek a hearing; only some exceptional cause, would, according to established custom, have warranted that.

Presently, just as the Commander absorbed in his reflections was on the point of turning aft in his promenade, he became sensible of Claggart's presence, and saw the doffed cap held in deferential expectancy. Here be it said that Captain Vere's personal knowledge of this petty-officer had only begun at the time of the ship's last sailing from home, Claggart then for the first, in transfer from a ship detained for repairs, supplying on board the *Indomitable* the place of a previous master-at-arms disabled and ashore.

No sooner did the Commander observe who it was that deferentially stood awaiting his notice, than a peculiar expression came over him. It was not unlike that which uncontrollably will flit across the countenance of one at unawares encountering a person who, though known to him indeed, has hardly been long enough known for thorough knowledge, but something in whose aspect nevertheless now for the first provokes a vaguely repellent distaste. But coming to a stand, and resuming much of his wonted official manner, save that a sort of impatience lurked in the intonation of the opening word, he said, "Well? what is it, Master-at-arms?"

With the air of a subordinate grieved at the necessity of being a messenger of ill tidings, and while conscientiously determined to be frank, yet equally resolved upon shunning overstatement, Claggart, at this invitation or rather summons to disburthen, spoke up. What he said, conveyed in the language of no uneducated man, was to the effect following, if not altogether in these words, namely, that during the chase and preparations for the possible encounter he had seen enough to convince him that at least one sailor aboard was a dangerous character in a ship mustering some who not only had taken a guilty part in the late serious troubles, but others also who, like the man in question, had entered His Majesty's service under another form than enlistment.

At this point Captain Vere with some impatience interrupted him: "Be direct, man; say impressed men."

Claggart made a gesture of subservience, and proceeded.

Quite lately he (Claggart) had begun to suspect that on the gun decks some sort of movement prompted by the sailor in question was covertly going on, but he had not thought himself warranted in reporting the suspicion so long as it remained indistinct. But from what he had that afternoon observed in the man referred to, the suspicion of something clandestine going on had advanced to a point less removed from certainty. He deeply felt, he added, the serious responsibility assumed in making a report involving such possible consequences to the individual mainly concerned, besides tending to augment those natural anxieties which every naval commander must feel in view of extraordinary outbreaks so recent as those which, he sorrowfully said it, it needed not to name.

Now at the first broaching of the matter Captain Vere, taken by surprise, could not wholly dissemble his disquietude. But as Claggart went on, the former's aspect changed into restiveness under something in the witness' manner in giving his testimony. However, he refrained from interrupting him. And Claggart, continuing, concluded with this: "God forbid, Your Honor, that the *Indomitable*'s should be the experience of the——"

"Never mind that!" here peremptorily broke in the superior, his face altering with anger, instinctively divining the ship that the other was about to name, one in which the Nore Mutiny had assumed a singularly tragical character that for a time jeopardized the life of its commander. Under the circumstances he was indignant at the purposed allusion. When the commissioned officers themselves were on all occasions very heedful how they referred to the recent events, for a petty-officer unnecessarily to allude to them in the presence of his Captain, this struck him as a most immodest presumption. Besides, to his quick sense of self-respect, it even looked under the circumstances something like an attempt to alarm him. Nor at first was he without some surprise that one who so far as he had hitherto come under his notice had shown considerable tact in his function should in this particular evince such lack of it.

But these thoughts and kindred dubious ones flitting across his mind were suddenly replaced by an intuitional surmise which, though as yet obscure in form, served practically to affect his reception of the ill tidings. Certain it is, that long versed in everything pertaining to the complicated gun-deck life, which like every other form of life, has its secret mines and dubious side, the side popularly disclaimed, Captain Vere did not permit himself to be unduly disturbed by the general tenor of his subordinate's report. Furthermore, if in view of recent events prompt action should be taken at the first palpable sign of recurring insubordination, for all that, not judicious would it be, he thought, to keep the idea of lingering disaffection alive by undue forwardness in crediting an informer, even if his own subordinate, and charged among other things with police surveillance of the crew. This feeling would not perhaps have so prevailed with him were it not that upon a prior occasion the patriotic zeal officially evinced by Claggart had somewhat irritated him as appearing rather supersensible and strained. Furthermore, something even in the official's self-possessed and somewhat ostentatious manner in making his specifications strangely reminded him of a bandsman, a perjurous witness in a capital case before a courtmartial ashore of which when a lieutenant, he, Captain Vere, had been a member.

Now the peremptory check given to Claggart in the matter of the arrested allusion was quickly followed up by this: "You say that there is at least one dangerous man aboard. Name him."

"William Budd. A foretopman, Your Honor—"

"William Budd," repeated Captain Vere with unfeigned astonishment; "and mean you the man that Lieutenant Ratcliff took from the merchantman not very long ago—the young fellow who seems to be so popular with the men—Billy, the 'Handsome Sailor,' as they call him?"

"The same, Your Honor; but for all his youth and good looks, a deep one. Not for nothing does he insinuate himself into the good will of his shipmates, since at the least all hands will at a pinch say a good word for him at all hazards. Did Lieutenant Ratcliff happen to tell Your Honor of that adroit fling of Budd's, jumping up in the cutter's bow under the merchantman's stern when he was being taken off? It is even masqued by that sort of good-humoured air that at heart he resents his impressment. You have but noted his fair cheek. A man-trap may be under his ruddy-tipped daisies."

Now the Handsome Sailor, as a signal figure among the crew, had naturally enough attracted the Captain's attention from the first. Tho' in general not very demonstrative to his officers, he had congratulated Lieutenant Ratcliff upon his good fortune in lighting on such a fine specimen of the genus homo, who in the nude might have posed for a statue of young Adam before the Fall.

As to Billy's adieu to the ship *Rights-of-Man*, which the boarding lieutenant had indeed reported to him, but in a deferential way more as a good story than aught else, Captain Vere, tho' mistakenly understanding it as a satiric sally, had but thought so much the better of the impressed man for it; as a military sailor, admiring the spirit that could take an arbitrary enlistment so merrily and sensibly. The Foretopman's conduct, too, so far as it had fallen under the Captain's notice, had confirmed the first happy augury, while the new recruit's qualities as a sailor–man seemed to be such that he had thought of recommending him to the executive officer for promotion to a place that would more frequently bring him under his own observation, namely, the captaincy of the mizzentop, replacing there in the starboard watch a man not so young whom partly for that reason he deemed less fitted for the post. Be it parenthesized here that since the mizzentopmen having not to handle such breadths of heavy canvas as the lower sails on the main-mast and fore-mast, a young man if of the right stuff not only seems best adapted to duty there, but in fact is generally selected for the captaincy of that top, and the company under him are light hands and often but striplings. In sum, Captain Vere had from the beginning deemed Billy Budd to be what in the naval parlance of the time was called a "King's bargain," that is to say, for His Britannic Majesty's Navy a capital investment at small outlay or none at all.

After a brief pause during which the reminiscences above mentioned passed vividly through his mind and he weighed the import of Claggart's last suggestion conveyed in the phrase "man-trap under his daisies," and the more he weighed it the less reliance he felt in the informer's good faith, suddenly he turned upon him and in a low voice: "Do you come to me, Master-at-arms, with so foggy a tale? As to Budd, cite me an act or spoken word of his confirmatory of what you in general charge against him. Stay," drawing nearer to him, "heed what you speak. Just now, and in a case like this, there is a yard-arm-end for the false-witness."

"Ah, Your Honor!" sighed Claggart, mildly shaking his shapely head as in sad deprecation of such unmerited severity of tone. Then, bridling—erecting himself as in virtuous self-assertion, he circumstantially alleged certain words and acts, which collectively, if credited, led to presumptions mortally inculpating Budd. And for some of these averments, he added, substantiating proof was not far.

With gray eyes impatient and distrustful essaying to fathom to the bottom Claggart's calm violet ones, Captain Vere again heard him out; then for the moment stood ruminating. The mood he evinced, Claggart—himself for the time liberated from the other's scrutiny—steadily regarded with a look difficult to render,—a look curious of the operation of his tactics, a look such as might have been that of the spokesman of the envious children of Jacob deceptively imposing upon the troubled patriarch the blood-dyed coat of young Joseph.

Though something exceptional in the moral quality of Captain Vere made him, in earnest encounter with a fellow-man, a veritable touch-stone of that man's essential nature, yet now as to Claggart and what was really going on in him, his feeling partook less of intuitional conviction than of strong suspicion clogged by strange dubieties. The perplexity he evinced proceeded less from aught touching the man informed against—as Claggart doubtless opined—than from considerations how best to act in regard to the informer. At first indeed he was naturally for summoning that substantiation of his allegations which Claggart said was at hand. But such a proceeding would result in the matter at once getting abroad, which in the present stage of it, he thought, might undesirably affect the ship's company. If Claggart was a false witness,—that closed the affair. And therefore before trying the accusation, he would first practically test the accuser; and he thought this could be done in a quiet undemonstrative way.

The measure he determined upon involved a shifting of the scene, a transfer to a place less exposed to observation than the broad quarter-deck. For although the few gun-room officers there at the time had, in due observance of naval etiquette, withdrawn to leeward the moment Captain Vere had begun his promenade on the deck's weather-side; and tho' during the colloquy with Claggart they of course ventured not to diminish the distance; and though throughout the interview Captain Vere's voice was far from high, and Claggart's silvery and low; and the wind in the cordage and the wash of the sea helped the more to put them beyond earshot; nevertheless, the interview's continuance already had attracted observation from some topmen aloft and other sailors in the waist or further forward.

Having determined upon his measures, Captain Vere forthwith took action. Abruptly turning to Claggart he asked, "Master-at-arms, is it now Budd's watch aloft?"

"No, Your Honor." Whereupon, "Mr. Wilkes!" summoning the nearest midshipman, "tell Albert to come to me." Albert was the Captain's hammock-boy, a sort of sea-valet in whose discretion and fidelity his master had much confidence. The lad appeared. "You know Budd the Foretopman?"

"I do, Sir."

"Go find him. It is his watch off. Manage to tell him out of earshot that he is wanted aft. Contrive it that he speaks to nobody. Keep him in talk yourself. And not till you get well aft here, not till then let him know that the place where he is wanted is my cabin. You understand. Go.—Master-at-arms, show yourself on the decks below, and when you think it time for Albert to be coming with his man, stand by quietly to follow the sailor in."

Now when the Foretopman found himself closeted there, as it were, in the cabin with the Captain and Claggart, he was surprised enough. But it was a surprise unaccompanied by apprehension or distrust. To an immature nature essentially honest and humane, forewarning intimations of subtler danger from one's kind come tardily if at all. The only thing that took shape in the young sailor's mind was this: Yes, the Captain, I have always thought, looks kindly upon me. Wonder if he's going to make me his coxswain. I should like that. And maybe now he is going to ask the Master-at-arms about me.

"Shut the door there, sentry," said the Commander; "stand without, and let nobody come in.—Now, Master-at-arms, tell this man to his face what you told of him to me"; and stood prepared to scrutinize the mutually confronting visages.

With the measured step and calm collected air of an asylum-physician approaching in the public hall some patient beginning to show indications of a coming paroxysm, Claggart deliberately advanced within short range of Billy, and mesmerically looking him in the eye, briefly recapitulated the accusation.

Not at first did Billy take it in. When he did, the rose-tan of his cheek looked struck as by white leprosy. He stood like one impaled and gagged. Meanwhile the accuser's eyes removing not as yet from the blue dilated ones, underwent a phenomenal change, their wonted rich violet color blurring into a muddy purple. Those lights of human intelligence losing human expression, gelidly protruding like the alien eyes of certain uncatalogued creatures of the deep. The first mesmeric glance was one of serpent fascination; the last was as the hungry lurch of the torpedo-fish.

"Speak, man!" said Captain Vere to the transfixed one, struck by his aspect even more than by Claggart's, "Speak! defend yourself." Which appeal caused but a strange dumb gesturing and gurgling in Billy; amazement at such an accusation so suddenly sprung on inexperienced nonage; this, and, it may be, horror of the accuser, serving to bring out his lurking defect and in this instance for the time intensifying it into a convulsed tongue-tie; while the intent head and entire form straining forward in an agony of ineffectual eagerness to obey the injunction to speak and defend himself, gave an expression to the face like that of a condemned Vestal priestess in the moment of being buried alive, and in the first struggle against suffocation.

Though at the time Captain Vere was quite ignorant of Billy's liability to vocal impediment, he now immediately divined it, since vividly Billy's aspect recalled to him that of a bright young schoolmate of his whom he had once seen struck by much the same startling impotence in the act of eagerly rising in the class to be foremost in response to a testing question put to it by the master. Going close up to the young sailor, and laying a soothing hand on his shoulder, he said, "There is no hurry, my boy. Take your time, take your time." Contrary to the effect intended, these words so fatherly in tone, doubtless touching Billy's heart to the quick, prompted yet more violent efforts at utterance—efforts soon ending for the time in confirming the paralysis, and bringing to his face an expression which was as a crucifixion to behold. The next instant, quick as the flame from a discharged cannon at night, his right arm shot out, and Claggart dropped to the deck. Whether intentionally or but owing to the young athlete's superior height, the blow had taken effect fully upon the forehead, so shapely and intellectual-looking a feature in the Master-at-arms; so that the body fell over lengthwise, like a heavy plank tilted from erectness. A gasp or two, and he lay motionless.

"Fated boy," breathed Captain Vere in tone so low as to be almost a whisper, "what have you done! But here, help me."

The twain raised the felled one from the loins up into a sitting position. The spare form flexibly acquiesced, but inertly. It was like handling a dead snake. They lowered it back. Regaining erectness Captain Vere with one hand covering his face stood to all appearance as impassive as the object at his feet. Was he absorbed in taking in all the bearings of the event and what was best not only now at once to be done, but also in the sequel? Slowly he uncovered his face; and the effect was as if the moon emerging from eclipse should reappear with quite another aspect than that which had gone into hiding. The father in him, manifested towards Billy thus far in the scene, was replaced by the military disciplinarian. In his official tone he bade the Foretopman retire to a state-room aft (pointing it out), and there remain till thence summoned. This order Billy in silence mechanically obeyed. Then going to the cabin-door where it opened on the quarter-deck, Captain Vere said to the sentry without, "Tell somebody to send Albert here." When the lad appeared his master so contrived it that he should not catch sight of the prone one. "Albert," he said to him, "tell the Surgeon I wish to see him. You need not come back till called." When the Surgeon entered—a self-poised character of that grave sense and experience that hardly anything could take him aback,—Captain Vere advanced to meet him, thus unconsciously intercepting his view of Claggart, and interrupting the other's wonted ceremonious salutation, said, "Nay, tell me how it is with yonder man," directing his attention to the prostrate one.

The Surgeon looked, and for all his self-command, somewhat started at the abrupt revelation. On Claggart's always pallid complexion, thick black blood was now oozing from nostril and ear. To the gazer's professional eye it was unmistakably no living man that he saw.

"Is it so then?" said Captain Vere intently watching him. "I thought it. But verify it." Whereupon the customary tests confirmed the Surgeon's first glance, who now looking up in unfeigned concern, cast a look of intense inquisitiveness upon his superior. But Captain Vere, with one hand to his brow, was standing motionless.

Suddenly, catching the Surgeon's arm convulsively, he exclaimed, pointing down to the body— "It is the divine judgement on Ananias! Look!"

Disturbed by the excited manner he had never before observed in the *Indomitable*'s Captain, and as yet wholly ignorant of the affair, the prudent Surgeon nevertheless held his peace, only again looking an earnest interrogation as to what it was that had resulted in such a tragedy.

But Captain Vere was now again motionless standing absorbed in thought. But again starting, he vehemently exclaimed—"Struck dead by an angel of God! Yet the angel must hang!"

At these passionate interjections, mere incoherences to the listener as yet unapprised of the antecedents, the Surgeon was profoundly discomposed. But now as recollecting himself, Captain Vere in less passionate tone briefly related the circumstances leading up to the event.

"But come; we must despatch," he added, "me to remove him" (meaning the body) "to yonder compartment," designating one opposite that where the Foretopman remained immured. Anew disturbed by a request that as implying a desire for secrecy, seemed unaccountably strange to him, there was nothing for the subordinate to do but comply.

"Go now," said Captain Vere with something of his wonted manner— "Go now. I shall presently call a drum-head court. Tell the lieutenants what has happened, and tell Mr. Mordant," meaning the Captain of Marines, "and charge them to keep the matter to themselves."

When I Was on the Frigate

[JÓN TRAUSTI]

I was stormbound in the fishing village. I had
come there by steamer, but now the steamer was
gone and I was left behind there, a stranger, at a
loss what to do.

My idea was to continue my journey overland,
and my route lay for the most part through the
mountainous country on the other side of the fjord.
I hadn't managed to hire horses or a guide, and it
was no easy matter to find one's own way in such
stormy weather when the rivers were running in full
flood. This was in the spring-time, round about the
beginning of May.

I was staying at the home of the local doctor, who
had given me shelter and who was now trying to
help me in every way he could. He was in my room
with me, and we were both sitting there, smoking

cigars and chatting together. I had given up all hope of continuing my journey that day and was making myself comfortable on the doctor's sofa. But when we least expected it, we heard the sound of heavy sea-boots clumping along the corridor, and there was a knock at the door.

Come in, said the doctor. The door opened slowly, and a young man in seamen's clothes stood in the doorway.

I was asked to tell you that old Hrolfur from Weir will take that chap over there across in his boat, if he likes, said the man, addressing himself to the doctor.

We both stood up, the doctor and I, and walked towards the door. That possibility hadn't occurred to either of us. Is old Hrolfur going fishing then? asked the doctor.

Yes, he's going out to the islands and staying there about a week. It won't make any difference to him to slip ashore at Muladalir, if it would be any help.

That's fine, said the doctor, turning to me. It's worth thinking over, unless you really need to go round the end of the fjord. It'll save you at least a day on your journey, and it'll be easier to get horses and a man in Muladalir than it is here.

This was all so unexpected that I didn't quite know what to say. I looked at the doctor and the stranger in turn, and my first thought was that the doctor was trying to get rid of me. Then it occurred to me what a fine thing it would be to avoid having to cross all those rivers which flow into the head of the fjord. Finally I decided that the doctor had no ulterior motive and that his advice was prompted by sheer goodwill.

Is old Hrolfur all right at the moment? the doctor asked the man in the doorway.

Yes, of course he is, said the man.

All right? I said, looking at them questioningly. I thought that was a funny thing to ask.

The doctor smiled.

He's just a bit queer—up here, he said, pointing to his forehead.

The thought of having to set out on a long sea journey with a man who was half crazy made me shudder. I am certain, too, that the doctor could see what I was thinking, for he smiled good-naturedly.

Is it safe to go with him then? I asked.

Oh yes, quite safe. He's not mad, far from it. He's just a bit queer—he's got 'bats in the belfry', as men say. He gets these attacks when he's at home in the dark winter days and has nothing to occupy him. But there's little sign of it in the summer. And he's a first-class seaman.

Yes, a first-class seaman who never fails, said the man in the doorway. It's quite safe to go on board with him now. You can take my word for that.

Are you going with him? asked the doctor. Yes, there's a crew of three with him. There'll be four of us in the boat altogether.

I looked at the man in the doorway—he was a young man of about twenty, promising and assured. I liked the look of him, very much.

Secretly I began to be ashamed of not daring to cross the fjord with three men such as he, even though the skipper was 'a bit queer in the head'.

Are you going to-day? said the doctor. Don't you think it's blowing a bit hard?

I don't think old Hrolfur'll let that bother him, said the man and smiled.

Can you use your sails?

Yes, I think so—there's a fair wind.

It was decided that I should go with them. I went to get ready as quickly as possible, and my luggage, saddle and bridle, were carried down to the boat.

The doctor walked to the jetty with us.

There, in the shelter of the breakwater, was old Hrolfur's boat, its mast already stepped, with the sail wrapped round it. It was a four-oared boat, rather bigger than usual, tarred all over except for the top plank, which was painted light blue. In the boat were the various bits of equipment needed for shark-fishing, including a thick wooden beam to which were attached four hooks of wrought iron, a keg of shark-bait which stank vilely, and barrels for the shark's liver. There were shark knives under the thwarts and huge gaffs hooked under the rib-boards. The crew had put the boxes containing their food and provisions in the prow.

In the stern could be seen the back of a man bending down. He was arranging stones in the well of the boat. He was dressed in overalls made of skin, which reached up to his armpits and which were fastened by pieces of thin rope crossing over his shoulders. Further forward there was a second man, and a third was up on the jetty.

Good day to you, Hrolfur, said the doctor.

Good day to you, grunted Hrolfur as he straightened himself up and spat a stream of yellowish-brown liquid from his mouth. Hand me that stone over there.

These last words were addressed not to the doctor or me, but to the man on the jetty. Hrolfur vouchsafed me one quick, unfriendly glance, but apart from that scarcely seemed to notice me. The look in those sharp, haunting eyes went through me like a knife. Never before had anyone looked at me with a glance so piercing and so full of misgiving.

He was a small man, and lively, though ageing fast. The face was thin, rather wrinkled, dark and weather-beaten, with light untidy wisps of hair round the mouth. I was immediately struck by a curious twitching in his features, perhaps a relic of former bouts of drinking. Otherwise his expression was harsh and melancholy. His hands were red, swollen and calloused as if by years of rowing.

Don't you think it's blowing rather hard, Hrolfur? asked the doctor after a long silence.

Oh, so-so, answered Hrolfur, without looking up.

Again there was silence. It was as if Hrolfur had neither time nor inclination for gossiping, even though it was the district medical officer talking to him.

The doctor looked at me and smiled. I was meant to understand that this was exactly what he had expected.

After another interval the doctor said: You are going to do this traveller a favour then, Hrolfur? Oh, well, the boat won't mind taking him.

In other words, I was to be nothing but so much ballast.

Don't you think it's going to be tricky landing there in Mular Creek?

Hrolfur straightened up, putting his hand to his back.

Oh, no, damn it, he said. There's an offshore wind and the sea's not bad, and anyway we'll probably get there with the incoming tide.

It isn't going to take you out of your way? I asked.

We won't argue about that. We'll get there all the same. We often give ourselves a rest in the old creek when we have to row.

Immediately afterwards I said good-bye to the doctor and slid down into the boat. The man on the jetty cast off, threw the rope down into the boat and jumped in after it.

One of the crew thrust the handle of an oar against the breakwater and pushed off. Then they rowed for a short spell to get into the wind, whilst old Hrolfur fixed the rudder.

The sail filled out; the boat heeled gently over and ran in a long curve. The islets at the harbour mouth rushed past us. We were making straight for the open bay.

On the horizon before us the mountainous cliffs, dark blue with a thick, ragged patch of mist at the top, towered steeply over the waves. In between, the sea stretched out, seemingly for miles.

Hrolfur was at the rudder. He sat back in the stern on a crossbeam flush with the gunwale, his feet braced against the ribs on either side and in his hands the rudder lines, one on each side, close to his thighs.

I was up with the crew near the mast. We all knew from experience that Icelandic boats sailed better when well-loaded forward. All four of us were lying down on the windward side, but to leeward the foam still bubbled up over the rowlocks.

If you think we're not going fast enough, lads, you'd better start rowing—but no extra pay, said old Hrolfur, grinning.

We all took his joke well, and I felt that it brought me nearer to the old man; up to then I'd been just a

little scared of him. A joke is always like an outstretched hand.

For a long time we hardly spoke. In front of the
mast we lay in silence, whilst old Hrolfur was at the
stern with the whole length of the boat between us.

The crew did all they could to make me comfortable. I lay on some soft sacking just in front of the
thwart and kept my head under the gunwale for
protection. The spray from the sea went right over
me and splashed down into the boat on the far side.

The boy who had come for me to the doctor's settled himself down in the bows in front of me. His
name was Eric Ericsson, and the more I saw of him
the more I liked him.

The second member of the crew sat crosswise over
the thwart with his back to the mast. He too was
young, his beard just beginning to grow, red-faced,
quiet and rather indolent-looking. He seemed completely indifferent, even though showers of spray
blew, one after another, straight into his face.

The third member of the crew lay down across the
boat behind the thwart; he put a folded oilskin jacket
under his head and fell asleep.

For a long time, almost an hour, I lay in silence,
thinking only of what I saw and heard around me.
There was more than enough to keep me awake.

I noticed how the sail billowed out, full of wind,
pulling hard at the clew-line, which was made fast to

the gunwale beside Hrolfur. The fore-sail resembled a beautifully curved sheet of steel, stiff and unyielding. Both sails were snow-white, semi-transparent and supple in movement, like the ivory sails on the model ships in Rosenborg Palace. The mast seemed to bend slightly and the stays were as taut as fiddle-strings. The boat quivered like a leaf. The waves pounded hard against the thin strakes of the boat's side. I could feel them on my cheek, though their dampness never penetrated; but in between these hammer blows their little pats were wonderfully friendly. Every now and then I could see the white frothing of the wave-crests above the gunwale, and sometimes under the sail the horizon was visible but, more often, there was nothing to be seen but the broad back of a wave, on which, for a time, the boat tossed before sinking down once more. The roll was scarcely noticeable, for the boat kept at the same angle all the time and cleft her way through the waves. The motion was comfortable and soothing to the mind; quite unlike the violent lunging of bigger ships.

Gradually the conversation came to life again. It was Eric who proved to be the most talkative, though the man on the thwart also threw in a word here and there.

We began to talk about old Hrolfur.

We spoke in a low voice so that he shouldn't hear what we said. There was, indeed, little danger of his doing so—the distance was too great and the storm was bound to carry our words away; but men always lower their voices when they speak of those they can see, even though they are speaking well of them.

My eyes scarcely left old Hrolfur, and as the men told me more, my picture of him became clearer and clearer.

He sat there silent, holding on to the steering ropes and staring straight ahead, not deigning us a single glance.

The crew's story was roughly this.

He was born and bred in the village, and he had never left it. The croft which he lived in was just opposite the weir in the river which flowed through the village, and was named after it.

He went to sea whenever possible; fished for shark in the spring and for cod and haddock in the other seasons. He never felt so happy as when he was on the sea; and if he couldn't go to sea, he sat alone at home in the croft mending his gear. He never went down to the harbour for work like the other fishermen and never worked on the land. Humming away and talking to himself he fiddled about in his shed, around his boat-house or his croft, his hands all grubby with tar and grease. If addressed, he was abrupt and curt in his answers, sometimes even abusive. Hardly anyone dared go near him.

Yet everyone liked him really. Everyone who got to know him said that he improved on acquaintance. His eccentricity increased as he grew older, but particularly after he had lost his son.

His son was already grown-up and had been a most promising young fellow. He was thought to be the most daring of all the skippers in the village and always went furthest out to sea; he was also the most successful fisherman of them all. But one day a sudden storm had caught them far out to sea, well outside the mouth of the fjord. Rowing hard, in the teeth of wind and tide, they managed to reach the cliffs, but by that time they were quite exhausted. Their idea had been to land at Mular Creek, but unfortunately their boat overturned as they tried to enter. Hrolfur's son and one other on board had been drowned, though the rest were saved.

After the disaster Hrolfur ignored everybody for a long time. It wasn't that he wept or lost heart. Perhaps he had done so for the first few days, but not afterwards. He just kept to himself. He took not the slightest notice of his wife and his other children, just as if they were no longer his concern. It was as though he felt he'd lost everything. He lived all alone with his sorrow and talked of it to no one. Nobody tried to question him; no one dared try to comfort him. Then, one winter, he started talking to himself.

Day and night, for a long time, he talked to himself, talked as though two or more men were chatting together, changing his tone of voice and acting in every way as though he were taking part in a lively and interesting conversation. There was nothing silly in what he said, although the subject matter was often difficult to follow. He would always answer if anyone spoke to him, slowly to be sure, but always sensibly and agreeably. Often, before he could answer, it was as though he had to wake up as from a sleep, and yet his work never suffered from these bouts of absentmindedness.

He never talked about his son. The conversations he held with himself were mostly concerned with various adventures he thought had befallen him; some were exaggerated, others pure invention. Sometimes he would talk of things he was going to do in the future, or things he would have done or ought to have in the past, but never about the present.

It wasn't long before the rumour spread that old Hrolfur was crazy, and for a long time hardly anyone dared to go to sea with him.

Now, that's all a thing of the past, said Eric and smiled. Nowadays there are always more who would like to go with him than he can take.

And does he catch plenty of fish?

Yes, he rarely fails.

Isn't he quite well-off then?

I don't know. At any rate he's not dependent on anyone else, and he's the sole owner of his boat and tackle.

He's rolling in money, the old devil, said the man at the mast, wiping the spray from his face with his hand.

Then they began to tell me about Mular Island and the life they would lead there in the coming week.

The island was a barren rock beyond the cliffs, and, in the autumn storms, was almost covered by the waves. The first thing they'd have to do, when they arrived, was to rebuild their refuge from the year before, roof it over with bits of driftwood and cover them with seaweed. That was to be their shelter at night, no matter what the weather. Nature had provided a landing-place, so that they'd no trouble with that, though the spot was so treacherous that one of them would have to stand watch over the boat every night.

Each evening they would row off from the island with their lines to some well-known fishing bank, for it was after midnight that the shark was most eager to take the bait. Savouring in his nostrils the smell of horse flesh soaked in rum and of rotten seal blubber, he would rush on the scent and greedily swallow whatever was offered. When he realised the sad truth that a huge hook with a strong barb was hidden inside this tempting dish and that it was no easy matter to disgorge the tasty morsel, he would try to gnaw through the shaft of the hook with his teeth. Very occasionally he might succeed, but usually his efforts failed. Attached to the hook was a length of strong iron chain; and sometimes, though defeated by the hook, he would manage to snip through the chain. Then, in his joy at being free, this creature with the magnificent appetite would immediately rush to the next hook, only to be caught there when the lines were drawn in. If the shark failed in his efforts to gnaw himself free, he would try, by twisting and turning, to break either the hook or the chain; but man had foreseen this possibility and had made the hook to turn with him. With exemplary patience 'the grey one' would continue his twisting until he had been drawn right up to the side of the boat and a second hook made fast in him. His sea-green, light-shy, pig-like eyes would glare malevolently up at his tormentors, and in his maddened fury he would bite, snap and fight until he almost capsized the boat.

For centuries our forefathers had hunted the shark like this in open boats, but nowadays men preferred to use decked vessels. No one in the district still used the old method, apart from old Hrolfur.

He had dragged in many a 'grey one'. From the bottom of the boat Eric picked up one of the hooks and passed it to me; it was of wrought iron, half an inch thick, with a point of cast steel. But the spinning joint was almost chewed through and the hook shaft bitten and gnawed—the 'grey one' had fought hard that time.

The crew told me so much about their fishing adventures that I longed to go to the island with them.

Suddenly Eric gave me a nudge.

The conversation stopped, and we all looked back at old Hrolfur.

Now he's talking to himself.

We all held our breath and listened.

Hrolfur sat like a statue, holding the rudder-lines. His eyes wore a far-away look and a curious smile of happiness played over his face.

After a short silence, he spoke again—in a perfectly normal voice.

When I was on the frigate—

For the time being that was all.

There was a touch of vanity in his smile, as though in memory of some old, half-ludicrous story from the past.

Yes, when I was on the frigate, my lad—

It was just as if there were someone sitting next to him beside the rudder, to whom he was relating his adventures.

Has he ever been on a warship? I whispered.

Never in his life, said Eric.

Our eyes never left him. I can still remember the curious twitching and working of his features. The eyes themselves were invisible; it was as though the man were asleep. But his forehead and temples were forever on the move, as if in mimicry of what he said.

I couldn't utter a sound. Everything was blurred before my eyes, for it was only then that the full realisation came upon me that the man at the rudder—the man who held all our lives in his hands—was half-crazed.

The crew nudged each other and chortled. They'd seen all this before.

She was running aground—heading straight for the reef,—a total loss, said Hrolfur, a total loss, I tell you. She was a beautiful craft, shining black and diced with white along the sides—ten fighting mouths on either side and a carved figure on her prow. I think the king would have been sorry to lose her. She was far too lovely to be ground to pieces there—they were glad when I turned up.

The crew did their best to smother their laughter.

'Top-sails up,' I shouted.—'Top-sails up, my lad.' The officer, for all his gold braid, went as pale as death. 'Top-sails up, in the devil's name.' The blue-jackets on the deck fell over themselves in fear. Yes, my lad, even though I hadn't a sword dangling by my side, I said, 'Top-sails up, in the devil's name.' And they obeyed me— they obeyed me. They didn't dare not to. 'Top-sails up, in the devil's name.'

Hrolfur raised himself up on the crossbeam, his fists clenched round the steering-ropes.

Eric was almost bursting with laughter and trying hard not to let it be heard; but the man at the mast made little attempt to stifle his.

She's made it, said Hrolfur, his face all smiles and nodding his head.—Out to sea. Straight out to sea. Let her lie down a bit, if she wants to. It'll do her no harm to ship a drop or two. Let it 'bubble up over her rowlocks,' as we Icelanders say. Even though she creaks a bit, it's all to the good. Her planks aren't rotten when they make that noise. All right, we'll sail the bottom out of her—but forward she'll go—forward, forward she shall go!

Hrolfur let his voice drop and drew out his words slowly.

By now we were far out in the fjord. The sea was rising and becoming more choppy because of tide currents. Good steering became more and more difficult. Hrolfur seemed to do it instinctively. He never once looked up and yet seemed to see all around him. He seemed to sense the approach of those bigger waves which had to be avoided or passed by. The general direction was never lost, but the boat ran wonderfully smoothly in and out of the waves—over them, before them and through them, as though she were possessed with human understanding. Not a single wave fell on her; they towered high above, advanced on her foaming and raging, but somehow—at the last moment—she turned aside. She was as sensitive as a frightened hind, quick to answer the rudder, as supple in her movements as a willing racehorse. Over her reigned the spirit of Hrolfur.

But Hrolfur himself was no longer there. He was 'on the frigate'. It was not his own boat he was steering in that hour, but a huge three-master with a whole cloud of sails above her and ten cannon on either side—a miracle of the shipwright's craft. The mainstays were of many-stranded steelwire, the halyards, all clustered together, struck at the mast and stays; they seemed inextricably tangled, and yet were in fact all ship-shape, taut and true, like the nerves in a human body. There was no need to steer her enormous bulk to avoid the waves or pass them by; it was enough to let her crush them with all her weight, let her grind them down and push them before her like drifts of snow. Groaning and creaking she ploughed straight on through all that came against her, heeling before the wind right down to her gunwale and leaving behind her a long furrow in the sea. High above the deck of this magnificent vessel, between two curved iron pillars, Hrolfur's boat hung like a tiny mussel shell.

Once upon a time this had been a dream of the future. But now that all hope of its fulfilment had been lost, the dream had long since become a reality. Hrolfur's adventure 'on the frigate' was a thing of the past.

For a long time he continued talking to himself, talked of how he had brought 'the frigate' safely to harbour, and how he had been awarded a 'gold medal' by the king. We could hear only snippets of this long rigmarole, but we never lost the drift of it. He spoke alternately in Danish and Icelandic, in many different tones of voice, and one could always tell, by the way he spoke, where he was in 'the frigate': whether he was addressing the crew on the deck, or the officers on the bridge, and when, his fantastic feat accomplished, he clinked glasses with them in the cabin on the poop.

The wind had slackened somewhat, but now that we had reached so far out into the bay the waves were higher; they were the remains of the huge ocean waves which raged on the high seas, remains which, despite the adverse wind, made their way far up the fjord.

Hrolfur no longer talked aloud, but he continued to hum quietly to himself. The crew around me began to doze off, and I think even I was almost asleep for a time. To tell the truth I wasn't very far from feeling seasick.

Soon afterwards the man who had been asleep in the space behind the mast rose to his feet, yawned once or twice, shook himself to restore his circulation and looked around.

It won't be long now before we get to Mular Creek, he said with his mouth still wide-open.

I was wide awake at once when I heard this, and raised myself up on my elbow. The mountain I had seen from the village—which then had been wrapped in a dark haze—now towered directly above us, rocky and enormous, with black sea-crags at its feet. The rocks were drenched with spray from the breakers, and the booming of the sea as it crashed into the basalt caves resounded like the roar of cannon.

There'll be no landing in the creek today, Hrolfur, the man said and yawned again. The breakers are too heavy.

Hrolfur pretended he hadn't heard.

Everybody aboard was awake now and watching the shore; and I think he was not the only one amongst us to shudder at the thought of landing.

On the mountain in front of us it was as though a panel was slowly moved to one side: the valleys of Muladalir opened up before us. Soon we glimpsed the roofs of the farms up on the hill-side. The beach itself was covered with rocks.

The boat turned into the inlet. It was quieter there than outside, and the sea was just a little another.

Loosen the foresail, Hrolfur ordered. It was Eric who obeyed and held on to the sheet. Hrolfur himself untied the mainsail, whilst at the same time keeping hold of the sheet. I imagined Hrolfur must be thinking it safer to have the sails loose as it was likely to be gusty in the inlet.

Are you going to sail in? said the man who'd been asleep. His voice came through a nose filled with snuff.

Shut up, said Hrolfur savagely.

The man took the hint and asked no more questions. No one asked a question, though every moment now was one of suspense.

We all gazed in silence at the cliffs, which were lathered in white foam.

One wave after another passed under the boat. They lifted her high up, as if to show us the surf. As the boat sank slowly down into the trough of the wave, the surf disappeared and with it much of the shore. The wave had shut it out.

I was surprised how little the boat moved, but an explanation of the mystery was soon forthcoming: the boat and all she carried were still subject to Hrolfur's will.

He let the wind out of the mainsail and, by careful manipulation of the rudder, kept the boat wonderfully still. He was standing up now in front of the crossbeam and staring fixedly out in front of the boat. He was no longer talking to himself, he was no longer 'on the frigate', but in his own boat; he knew well how much depended on him.

After waiting for a while, watching his opportunity, Hrolfur suddenly let her go at full speed once more.

Now the moment had come—a moment I shall never forget—nor probably any of us who were in the boat with him. It was not fear that gripped us but something more like excitement before a battle. Yet, if the choice had been mine, we should have turned back from the creek that day.

Hrolfur stood at the rudder, immovable, his eyes shifting from side to side, now under the sail, now past it. He chewed vigorously on his quid of tobacco and spat. There was much less sign now of the twitchings round his eyes than there'd been earlier in the day, and his very calmness had a soothing effect on us all.

As we approached the creek, a huge wave rose up behind us. Hrolfur glanced at it with the corner of his eye. He spat and bared his teeth. The wave rose and rose, and it reached us just at the mouth of the creek, its overhanging peak so sharp as to be almost transparent. It seemed to be making straight for the boat.

As I watched, I felt the boat plummet down, as if the sea was snatched from under her; it was the under-tow—the wave was drawing the waters back beneath it. By the gunwale the blue-green sea frothed white as it poured back from the skerries near the entrance to the creek.

The boat almost stood on end; it was as if the sea was boiling around us—boiling until the very seaweed on the rocks was turned to broth.

Suddenly an ice-cold lash, as of a whip, seemed to strike me in the face. I staggered forwards under the blow and grasped at one of the mainstays.

Let go the foresail, shouted Hrolfur.

When I was able to look up, the sails were flapping idly over the gunwale. The boat floated gently into the creek, thwart-deep in water.

We all felt fine.

It's true, I could feel the cold sea water dripping down my bare back, underneath my shirt, but I didn't mind. All that had happened to me was but a kiss, given me in token of farewell by the youngest daughter of the goddess of the waves.

The boat floated slowly in on the unaccustomed calm of the waters and stopped at the landing-place.

Standing there watching were two men from the farm.

I thought as much, it had to be old Hrolfur, one of them called out as we landed. It's no ordinary man's job to get into the creek on a day like this.

Hrolfur's face was wreathed in smiles: he made no answer, but slipping off the rudder in case it should touch bottom he laid it down across the stern.

We were given a royal welcome by the fanners from Mular, and all that I needed to further me on my journey was readily available and willingly granted. Nowhere does Iceland's hospitality flourish so well as in her outlying stations and in the remotest of her valleys, where travellers are few.

We all got out of the boat and pulled her clear of the waves. Every one of us was only too glad to get the opportunity of stretching his legs after sitting cramped up on the hard boards for nearly four hours.

I walked up to where old Hrolfur stood apart, on the low, flat rocks, thanked him for the trip and asked him what it cost.

Cost? he said, scarce looking at me. What does it cost? Just a minute now, my lad,—just a minute.

He answered me with the complete lack of formality one accords an old friend, though we had met for the first time that day. His whole face was scowling now, as he answered me brusquely—indeed, almost curtly; and yet there was something attractive about him, something that aroused both trust and respect and which made it impossible for me to resent his familiarity.

How much the trip costs? Just a minute now.

It seemed that his thoughts were elsewhere. He unloosened the brace of his overalls, reached down into the pocket of his patched garments beneath and, drawing out a fine length of chewing tobacco, took a bite. Then, breaking off a smallish length, he dropped it into the crown of his seaman's hat. Finally, slowly and very deliberately, he refastened the top of his overalls.

I expect you got a bit wet out there coming into the creek.

Oh, not really.

Sometimes one gets unpleasantly damp out there.

Hrolfur stood still, chewing his quid of tobacco and staring out at the entrance to the creek. He seemed to have forgotten all about answering my question.

Sometimes one gets unpleasantly damp out there, he repeated, laying great emphasis on every word. I looked straight at him and saw there were tears in his eyes. Now his features were all working again and twitching as they had done earlier.

There's many a boat filled up there, he added, and some have got no further. But I've floated in and out so far. Oh well, 'The silver cup sinks, but the wooden bowl floats on', as the proverb says. There was a time when I had to drag out of the water here a man who was better than me in every way—that's when I really got to know the old creek.

For a time he continued to stand there, staring out at the creek without saying a word. But, at last, after wiping the tears from his face with the back of his glove, he seemed to come to himself once more.

You were asking, my lad, what the journey costs—
it costs nothing.

Nothing? What nonsense!

Not since you got wet, said Hrolfur and smiled,
though you could still see the tears in his eyes. It's an
old law of ours that if the ferry-man lets his passengers get wet, even though it's only their big toe, then
he forfeits his toll.

I repeatedly begged Hrolfur to let me pay him for
the journey, but it was no use. At last he became serious again and said:

The journey costs nothing, as I said to you. I've
brought many a traveller over here to the creek and
never taken a penny in return. But if you ever come
back to our village again, and old Hrolfur should
happen to be on land, come over to Weir and drink
a cup of coffee with him—black coffee with brown
rock-sugar and a drop of brandy in it; that is, if you
can bring yourself to do such a thing.

This I promised him, and old Hrolfur shook me
firmly and meaningfully by the hand as we parted.

As they prepared to leave, we all three, the farmers
from Mular and I, stood there on the rocks to see how
Hrolfur would manage. The crew had furled the sails
and sat down to the oars, whilst old Hrolfur stood in
front of the crossbeam, holding the rudder-line.

They weren't rowing though, but held their oars
up, waiting for their opportunity. All this while,

wave after wave came riding through the entrance to the creek, pouring their white cascades of foam over the reefs.

Hrolfur watched them steadily and waited, like an animal ready to pounce on its prey.

Now, my lads, cried Hrolfur suddenly. The oars crashed into the sea, and the boat shot forward.

Just so, I thought, must the Vikings in olden time have rowed to the attack.

Hrolfur's voice was lost to us in the roaring of the surf, but he seemed to be urging the men on to row their utmost. They rowed, indeed, like things possessed, and the boat hurtled forward. At the mouth of the creek a surf-topped wave rose against them, sharp and concave, as it rushed on its way to the reefs. We held our breath. It was a terrifying but magnificent sight.

Hrolfur shouted something loudly, and at the same moment every oar hugged the side of the boat, like the fins of a salmon as it hurls itself at a waterfall. The boat plunged straight into the wave. For a moment we lost sight of her in the swirling spray; only the mast was visible. When we saw her again, she was well out past the breakers. She'd been moving fast and was well steered.

Hrolfur took his place on the crossbeam as if nothing had happened, just as he had sat there earlier in the day, whilst he was 'on the frigate'.

Two of the crew began to set the sails, whilst one started to bail out. Soon the boat was once more on the move.

I felt a strange lump in my throat as I watched old Hrolfur sailing away.

God bless you, old salt, I thought. You thoroughly deserved to cleave through the cold waters of Iceland in a shapely frigate.

The boat heeled over gracefully and floated over the waves like a gull with its wings outstretched. We stood there watching, without a move, until she disappeared behind the headland.

The Rescue

[RICHARD HAKLUYT]

Among our merchants here in England, it is a common voyage to 'traffic to Spain; whereunto a ship called the *Three Half Moons*, manned with eight and thirty men, well fenced with munitions, the better to encounter their enemies withal, and having wind and tide, set from Portsmouth 1563, and bended her journey towards Seville, a city in Spain, intending there to traffic with them. And falling near the Straits, they perceived themselves to be beset round about with eight galleys of the Turks, in such wise that there was no way for them to fly or to escape away, but that either they must yield or else be sunk, which the owner perceiving, manfully encouraged his company, exhorting them valiantly to show their manhood, showing them that God was their God, and not their enemies', requesting them also not to faint in seeing such a heap of their enemies ready to devour them; putting them in mind also, that if it were God's pleasure to give them into their enemies' hands, it was not they that ought to show one displeasant look or countenance there against; but to take it patiently, and not to prescribe a day and time for their deliverance, as the citizens of Bethulia did, but to put themselves under His mercy. And again, if it were His mind and good will to show His mighty power by them, if their enemies were ten times so many, they were not able to stand in their hands; putting them, likewise, in mind of the old and ancient worthiness of their countrymen, who in the hardest extremities have always most prevailed, and gone away conquerors; yea, and where it hath been almost impossible. "Such," quoth he, "hath been the valiantness of our countrymen, and such hath been the mighty power of our God."

With such other like encouragements, exhorting them to behave themselves manfully, they fell all on their knees, making their prayers briefly unto God; who, being all risen up again, perceived their enemies, by their signs and defiances, bent to the spoil, whose mercy was nothing else but cruelty; whereupon every man took him to his weapon.

Then stood up one Grove, the master, being a comely man, with his sword and target, holding them up in defiance against his enemies. So likewise stood up the owner, the master's mate, boatswain, purser, and every man well appointed. Now likewise sounded up the drums, trumpets, and flutes, which would have encouraged any man, had he never so little heart or courage in him.

Then taketh him to his charge John Fox, the gunner, in the disposing of his pieces, in order to the best effect, and, sending his bullets towards the Turks, who likewise bestowed their pieces thrice as fast towards the Christians. But shortly they drew near, so that the bowmen fell to their charge in sending forth their arrows so thick amongst the galleys, and also in doubling their shot so sore upon the galleys, that there were twice so many of the Turks slain as the number of the Christians were in all. But the Turks discharged twice as fast against the Christians, and so long, that the ship was very sore stricken and bruised under water; which the Turks, perceiving, made the more haste to come aboard the ship: which, ere they could do, many a Turk bought it dearly with the loss of their lives. Yet was all in vain; boarded they were, where they found so hot a skirmish, that it had been better they had not meddled with the feast; for the Englishmen showed themselves men indeed, in working manfully with their brown bills and halberds, where the owner, master, boatswain, and their company stood to it so lustily, that the Turks were half dismayed. But chiefly the boatswain showed himself valiant above the rest, for he fared amongst the Turks like a wood lion; for there was none of them that either could or durst stand in his face, till at last there came a shot from the Turks which brake his whistle asunder, and smote him on the breast, so that he fell down, bidding them farewell, and to be of good comfort, encouraging them, likewise, to win praise by death, rather than to live captives in misery and shame, which they, hearing, indeed, intended to have done, as it appeared by their skirmish; but the press and store of the Turks were so great, that they were not long able to endure, but were so overpressed, that they could not wield their weapons, by reason whereof they must needs be taken, which none of them intended to have been, but rather to have died, except only the master's mate, who shrunk from the skirmish, like a notable coward, esteeming neither the value of his name, nor accounting of the present example of his fellows, nor having respect to the miseries whereunto he should be put.

But in fine, so it was, that the Turks were victors, whereof they had no great cause to rejoice or triumph. Then would it have grieved any hard heart to see these infidels so violently entreating the Christians, not having any respect of their manhood, which they had tasted of, nor yet respecting their own state, how they might have met with such a booty as might have given them the overthrow; but

no remorse hereof, or anything else doth bridle their
fierce and tyrannous dealing, but the Christians must
needs to the galleys, to serve in new offices; and they
were no sooner in them, but their garments were
pulled over their ears, and torn from their backs, and
they set to the oars.

I will make no mention of their miseries, being
now under their enemies' raging stripes. I think there
is no man will judge their fare good, or their bodies
unloaden of stripes, and not pestered with too much
heat, and also with too much cold; but I will go to
my purpose, which is to show the end of those being
in mere misery, which continually do call on God
with a steadfast hope that He will deliver them, and
with a sure faith that He can do it.

Nigh to the city of Alexandria, being a haven
town, and under the dominion of the Turks, there is
a road, being made very fencible with strong walls,
whereinto the Turks do customably bring their galleys on shore every year, in the winter season, and
there do trim them, and lay them up against the
spring-time; in which road there is a prison, wherein
the captives and such prisoners as serve in the galleys
are put for all that time, until the seas be calm and
passable for the galleys, every prisoner being most
grievously laden with irons on their legs, to their
great pain, and sore disabling of them to any labour;
into which prison were these Christians put and fast

warded all the winter season. But ere it was long, the master and the owner, by means of friends, were redeemed, the rest abiding still in the misery, while that they were all, through reason of their ill-usage and worse fare, miserably starved, saving one John Fox, who (as some men can abide harder and more misery than other some can, so can some likewise make more shift, and work more duties to help their state and living, than other some can do) being somewhat skilful in the craft of a barber, by reason thereof made great shift in helping his fare now and then with a good meal. Insomuch, till at the last God sent him favour in the sight of the keeper of the prison, so that he had leave to go in and out to the road at his pleasure, paying a certain stipend unto the keeper, and wearing a lock about his leg, which liberty likewise five more had upon like sufferance, who, by reason of their long imprisonment, not being feared or suspected to start aside, or that they would work the Turks any mischief, had liberty to go in and out at the said road, in such manner as this John Fox did, with irons on their legs, and to return again at night.

In the year of our Lord 1577, in the winter season, the galleys happily coming to their accustomed harbourage, and being discharged of all their masts, sails, and other such furnitures as unto galleys do appertain, and all the masters and mariners of them being then nested in their own homes, there remained in the prison of the said road two hundred three score and eight Christian prisoners who had been taken by the Turks' force, and were of fifteen sundry nations. Among which there were three Englishmen, whereof one was named John Fox, of Woodbridge, in Suffolk, the other William Wickney, of Portsmouth, in the county of Southampton, and the third Robert Moore, of Harwich, in the county of Essex; which John Fox, having been thirteen or fourteen years under their gentle entreatance, and being too weary thereof, minding his escape, weighed with himself by what means it might be brought to pass, and continually pondering with himself thereof, took a good heart unto him, in the hope that God would not be always scourging His children, and never ceasing to pray Him to further his intended enterprise, if that it should redound to His glory.

Not far from the road, and somewhat from thence, at one side of the city, there was a certain victualling house, which one Peter Vuticaro had hired, paying also a certain fee unto the keeper of the road. This Peter Vuticaro was a Spaniard born, and a Christian, and had been prisoner above thirty years, and never practised any means to escape, but kept himself quiet without touch or suspect of any conspiracy, until that now this John Fox using much thither, they brake one to another their minds, concerning the restraint of their liberty and imprisonment. So that this John Fox, at length opening unto this Vuticaro the device which he would fain put in practice, made privy one more to this their intent; which three debated of this matter at such times as they could compass to meet together, insomuch that, at seven weeks' end they had sufficiently concluded how the matter should be, if it pleased God to further them thereto; who, making five more privy to this their device, whom they thought that they might safely trust, determined in three nights after to accomplish their deliberate purpose. Whereupon the same John Fox and Peter Vuticaro, and the other five appointed to meet all together in the prison the next day, being the last day of December, where this John Fox certified the rest of the prisoners what their intent and device was, and how and when they minded to bring that purpose to pass, who thereunto persuaded them without much ado to further their device; which, the same John Fox seeing, delivered unto them a sort of files, which he had gathered together for this purpose by the means of Peter Vuticaro, charging them that every man should be ready, discharged of his irons, by eight of the clock on the next day at night.

On the next day at night, the said John Fox, and his five other companions, being all come to the house of Peter Vuticaro, passing the time away in mirth for fear of suspect till the night came on, so that it was time for them to put in practice their device, sent Peter Vuticaro to the master of the road, in the name of one of the masters of the city, with whom this keeper was acquainted, and at whose request he also would come at the first; who desired him to take the pains to meet him there, promising him that he would bring him back again. The keeper agreed to go with him, asking the warders not to bar the gate, saying that he would not stay long, but would come again with all speed.

In the mean-season, the other seven had provided them of such weapons as they could get in that house, and John Fox took him to an old rusty sword-blade without either hilt or pommel, which he made to serve his turn in bending the hand end of the sword instead of a pommel, and the other had got such spits and glaves as they found in the house.

The keeper being now come unto the house, and perceiving no light nor hearing any noise, straightway suspected the matter; and returning backward, John Fox, standing behind the corner of the house, stepped forth unto him; who, perceiving it to be John Fox, said, "O Fox, what have I deserved of thee that thou shouldest seek my death?"

"Thou villain," quoth Fox, "hast been a bloodsucker of many a Christian's blood, and now thou shalt know what thou hast deserved at my hands," wherewith he lift up his bright shining sword of ten

years' rust, and stroke him so main a blow, as there-
withal his head clave asunder so that he fell stark
dead to the ground. Whereupon Peter Vuticaro went
in and certified the rest how the case stood with the
keeper, and they came presently forth, and some
with their spits ran him through, and the other with
their glaves hewed him in sunder, cut off his head,
and mangled him so that no man should discern
what he was.

Then marched they toward the road, whereinto
they entered softly, where were five warders, whom
one of them asked, saying, who was there? Quoth
Fox and his company, "All friends." Which when
they were all within proved contrary; for, quoth Fox,
"My masters, here is not to every man a man, wherefore look you, play your parts." Who so behaved
themselves indeed, that they had despatched these
five quickly. Then John Fox, intending not to be
barren of his enterprise, and minding to work surely
in that which he went about, barred the gate surely,
and planted a cannon against it.

Then entered they into the jailer's lodge, where
they found the keys of the fortress and prison by his
bedside, and there got they all better weapons. In
this chamber was a chest wherein was a rich treasure,
and all in ducats, which this Peter Vuticaro and two
more opening, stuffed themselves so full as they
could between their shirts and their skin; which John

Fox would not once touch and said, "that it was his and their liberty which he fought for, to the honour of his God, and not to make a mart of the wicked treasure of the infidels." Yet did these words sink nothing unto their stomachs; they did it for a good intent. So did Saul save the fattest oxen to offer unto the Lord, and they to serve their own turn. But neither did Saul scape the wrath of God therefor, neither had these that thing which they desired so, and did thirst after. Such is God's justice. He that they put their trust in to deliver them from the tyrannous hands of their enemies, he, I say, could supply their want of necessaries.

Now these eight, being armed with such weapons as they thought well of, thinking themselves sufficient champions to encounter a stronger enemy, and coming unto the prison, Fox opened the gates and doors thereof, and called forth all the prisoners, whom he set, some to ramming up the gate, some to the dressing up of a certain galley which was the best in all the road, and was called "The Captain of Alexandria," whereinto some carried masts, sails, oars, and other such furniture, as doth belong unto a galley.

At the prison were certain warders whom John Fox and his company slew, in the killing of whom there were eight more of the Turks which perceived them, and got them to the top of the prison, unto whom John Fox and his company were fain to come by ladders, where they found a hot skirmish, for some of them were there slain, some wounded, and some but scarred and not hurt. As John Fox was thrice shot through his apparel, and not hurt, Peter Vuticaro and the other two, that had armed them with the ducats, were slain, as not able to wield themselves, being so pestered with the weight and uneasy carrying of the wicked and profane treasure; and also divers Christians were as well hurt about that skirmish as Turks slain.

Amongst the Turks was one thrust through, who (let us not say that it was ill-fortune) fell off from the top of the prison wall, and made such a groaning that the inhabitants thereabout (as here and there stood a house or two), came and questioned him, so that they understood the case, how that the prisoners were paying their ransoms; wherewith they raised both Alexandria, which lay on the west side of the road, and a castle which was at the city's end next to the road, and also another fortress which lay on the north side of the road, so that now they had no way to escape but one, which by man's reason (the two holds lying so upon the mouth of the road) might seem impossible to be a way for them. So was the Red Sea impossible for the Israelites to pass through, the hills and rocks lay so on the one side, and their enemies compassed them on the other. So was it impossible that the walls of Jericho should fall down, being neither undermined nor yet rammed at with engines, nor yet any man's wisdom, policy, or help, set or put thereunto. Such impossibilities can our God make possible. He that held the lion's jaws from rending Daniel asunder, yea, or yet from once touching him to his hurt, cannot He hold the roaring cannons of this hellish force? He that kept the fire's rage in the hot burning oven from the three children that praised His name, cannot He keep the fire's flaming blasts from among His elect?

Now is the road fraught with lusty soldiers, labourers, and mariners, who are fain to stand to their tackling, in setting to every man his hand, some to the carrying in of victuals, some munitions, some oars, and some one thing some another, but most are keeping their enemy from the wall of the road. But to be short, there was no time misspent, no man idle, nor any man's labour ill-bestowed or in vain. So that in short time this galley was ready trimmed up. Whereinto every man leaped in all haste, hoisting up the sails lustily, yielding themselves to His mercy and grace, in Whose hands is both wind and weather.

Now is this galley a-float, and out of the shelter of the road; now have the two castles full power upon the galley; now is there no remedy but to sink. How can it be avoided? The cannons let fly from both sides, and the galley is even in the middest and between them both. What man can devise to save it? There is no man but would think it must needs be sunk.

There was not one of them that feared the shot which went thundering round about their ears, nor yet were once scarred or touched with five and forty shot which came from the castles. Here did God hold forth His buckler, He shieldeth now this galley, and hath tried their faith to the uttermost. Now cometh His special help; yea, even when man thinks them past all help, then cometh He Himself down from Heaven with His mighty power, then is His present remedy most ready. For they sail away, being not once touched by the glance of a shot, and are quickly out of the Turkish cannons' reach. Then might they see them coming down by heaps to the water's side, in companies like unto swarms of bees, making show to come after them with galleys, bustling themselves to dress up the galleys, which would be a swift piece of work for them to do, for that they had neither oars, masts, sails, nor anything else ready in any galley. But yet they are carrying into them, some into one galley, and some into another, so that, being such a confusion amongst them, without any certain guide, it were a thing impossible to overtake the Christians; beside that, there was no man that would take charge of a galley, the weather was so rough, and there was such an amazedness amongst them. And verily, I think their God was amazed thereat; it could not be but that he must blush for shame, he can speak never a word for dullness, much less can he help them in such an extremity. Well, howsoever it is, he is very much to blame to suffer them to receive such a gibe. But howsoever their God behaved himself, our God showed Himself a God indeed, and that He was the only living God; for the seas were swift under His faithful, which made the enemies aghast to behold them; a skilfuller pilot leads them, and their mariners bestir them lustily; but the Turks had neither mariners, pilot, nor any skilful master, that was in readiness at this pinch.

When the Christians were safe out of the enemy's coast, John Fox called to them all, telling them to be thankful unto Almighty God for their delivery, and most humbly to fall down upon their knees, beseeching Him to aid them to their friends' land, and not to bring them into another danger, since He had most mightily delivered them from so great a thraldom and bondage.

Thus when every man had made his petition, they fell straightway to their labour with the oars, in helping one another when they were wearied, and with great labour striving to come to some Christian land, as near as they could guess by the stars. But the winds were so contrary, one while driving them this way, another while that way, so that they were now in a new maze, thinking that God had forsaken them and left them to a greater danger. And forasmuch as there were no victuals now left in the galley, it might have been a cause to them (if they had been the Israelites), to have murmured against their God; but they knew how that their God, who had delivered Egypt, was such a loving and merciful God, as that He would not suffer them to be confounded in whom He had wrought so great a wonder, but what calamity soever they sustained, they knew it was but for their further trial, and also (in putting them in mind of their further misery), to cause them not to triumph and glory in themselves therefor. Having, I say, no victuals in the galley, it might seem one misery continually to fall upon another's neck; but to be brief the famine grew to be so great that in twenty-eight days, wherein they were on the sea, there died eight persons, to the astonishment of all the rest.

So it fell out that upon the twenty-ninth day after they set from Alexandria, they fell on the isle of Candia, and landed at Gallipoli, where they were made much of by the abbot and monks there, who caused them to stay there while they were well refreshed and eased. They kept there the sword wherewith John Fox had killed the keeper, esteeming it as a most precious relic, and hung it up for a monument.

When they thought good, having leave to depart from thence, they sailed along the coast till they arrived at Tarento, where they sold their galley, and divided

it, every man having a part thereof. The Turks on re-
ceiving so shameful a foil at their hands, pursued the
Christians, and scoured the seas, where they could
imagine that they had bent their course. And the
Christians had departed from thence on the one day
in the morning and seven galleys of the Turks came
thither that night, as it was certified by those who
followed Fox and his company, fearing lest they
should have been met with. And then they came
afoot to Naples, where they departed asunder, every
man taking him to his next way home. From
whence John Fox took his journey unto Rome,
where he was well entertained by an Englishman
who presented his worthy deed unto the Pope, who
rewarded him liberally, and gave him letters unto the
King of Spain, where he was very well entertained
of him there, who for this his most worthy enterprise
gave him in fee twenty pence a day. From whence,
being desirous to come into his own country, he
came thither at such time as he conviently could,
which was in the year of our Lord God 1579; who
being come into England went unto the Court, and
showed all his travel unto the Council, who considering of the state of this man, in that he had spent
and lost a great part of his youth in thraldom and
bondage, extended to him their liberality to help to
maintain him now in age, to their right honour and
to the encouragement of all true-hearted Christians.

The Wreck of the Golden Mary

[CHARLES DICKENS]

We had room for twenty passengers. Our sailing advertisement was no sooner out, than we might have taken these twenty times over. In entering our men, I and John (both together) picked them, and we entered none but good hands—as good as were to be found in that port. And so, in a good ship of the best build, well owned, well arranged, well officered, well manned, well found in all respects, we parted with our pilot at a quarter past four o'clock in the afternoon of the seventh of March, one thousand eight hundred and fifty-one, and stood with a fair wind out to sea.

It may be easily believed that up to that time I had had no leisure to be intimate with my passengers. The most of them were then in their berths sea-sick;

however, in going among them, telling them what was good for them, persuading them not to be there, but to come up on deck and feel the breeze, and in rousing them with a joke, or a comfortable word, I made acquaintance with them, perhaps, in a more friendly and confidential way from the first, than I might have done at the cabin table.

Of my passengers, I need only particularise, just at present, a bright-eyed blooming young wife who was going out to join her husband in California, taking with her their only child, a little girl of three years old, whom he had never seen; a sedate young woman in black, some five years older (about thirty as I should say), who was going out to join a brother; and an old gentleman, a good deal like a hawk if his eyes had been better and not so red, who was always talking, morning, noon, and night, about the gold discovery. But, whether he was making the voyage, thinking his old arms could dig for gold, or whether his speculation was to buy it, or to barter for it, or to cheat for it, or to snatch it anyhow from other people, was his secret. He kept his secret.

These three and the child were the soonest well. The child was a most engaging child, to be sure, and very fond of me: though I am bound to admit that John Steadiman and I were borne on her pretty little looks in reverse order, and that he was captain there, and I was mate. It was beautiful to watch her with

John, and it was beautiful to watch John with her. Few would have thought it possible, to see John playing at bo-peep round the mast, that he was the man who had caught up an iron bar and struck a Malay and a Maltese dead, as they were gliding with their knives down the cabin stair aboard the barque *Old England*, when the captain lay ill in his cot, off Saugar Point. But he was; and give him his back against a bulwark, he would have done the same by half a dozen of them. The name of the young mother was Mrs. Atherfield, the name of the young lady in black was Miss Coleshaw, and the name of the old gentleman was Mr. Rarx.

As the child had a quantity of shining fair hair, clustering in curls all about her face, and as her name was Lucy, Steadiman gave her the name of the Golden Lucy. So, we had the Golden Lucy and the *Golden Mary*; and John kept up the idea to that extent as he and the child went playing about the decks, that I believe she used to think the ship was alive somehow—a sister or companion, going to the same place as herself. She liked to be by the wheel, and in fine weather, I have often stood by the man whose trick it was at the wheel, only to hear her, sitting near my feet, talking to the ship. Never had a child such a doll before, I suppose; but she made a doll of the *Golden Mary*, and used to dress her up by tying ribbons and little bits of finery to the belaying-pins; and nobody ever moved them, unless it was to save them from being blown away.

Of course I took charge of the two young women, and I called them "my dear," and they never minded, knowing that whatever I said was said in a fatherly and protecting spirit. I gave them their places on each side of me at dinner, Mrs. Atherfield on my right and Miss Coleshaw on my left; and I directed the unmarried lady to serve out the breakfast, and the married lady to serve out the tea. Likewise I said to my black steward in their presence, "Tom Snow, these two ladies are equally the mistresses of this house, and do you obey their orders equally;" at which Tom laughed, and they all laughed.

Old Mr. Rarx was not a pleasant man to look at, nor yet to talk to, or to be with, for no one could help seeing that he was a sordid and selfish character, and that he had warped further and further out of the straight with time. Not but what he was on his best behaviour with us, as everybody was; for we had no bickering among us, for'ard or aft. I only mean to say, he was not the man one would have chosen for a messmate. If choice there had been, one might even have gone a few points out of one's course, to say, "No! Not him!" But, there was one curious inconsistency in Mr. Rarx. That was, that he took an astonishing interest in the child. He looked, and I may add, he was, one of the last of men to care at all for a child, or to care much for any human creature. Still, he went so far as to be habitually uneasy, if the child was long on deck, out of his sight. He was always afraid of her falling overboard, or falling down a hatchway, or of a block or what not coming down upon her from the rigging in the working of the ship, or of her getting some hurt or other. He used to look at her and touch her, as if she was something precious to him. He was always solicitous about her not injuring her health, and constantly entreated her mother to be careful of it. This was so much the more curious, because the child did not like him, but used to shrink away from him, and would not even put out her hand to him without coaxing from others. I believe that every soul on board frequently noticed this, and not one of us understood it. However, it was such a plain fact, that John Steadiman said more than once when old Mr. Rarx was not within earshot, that if the *Golden Mary* felt a tenderness for the dear old gentleman she carried in her lap, she must be bitterly jealous of the Golden Lucy.

Before I go any further with this narrative, I will state that our ship was a barque of three hundred tons, carrying a crew of eighteen men, a second mate in addition to John, a carpenter, an armourer or smith, and two apprentices (one a Scotch boy, poor little fellow). We had three boats; the Long-boat, capable of carrying twenty-five men; the Cutter, capable of carrying fifteen; and the Surf-boat, capable of carrying ten. I put down the capacity of these boats according to the numbers they were really meant to hold.

We had tastes of bad weather and head-winds, of course; but, on the whole we had as fine a run as any reasonable man could expect, for sixty days. I then began to enter two remarks in the ship's Log and in my Journal; first, that there was an unusual and amazing quantity of ice; second, that the nights were most wonderfully dark, in spite of the ice.

For five days and a half, it seemed quite useless and hopeless to alter the ship's course so as to stand out of the way of this ice. I made what southing I could; but, all that time, we were beset by it. Mrs. Atherfield after standing by me on deck once, looking for some time in an awed manner at the great bergs that surrounded us, said in a whisper, "O! Captain Ravender, it looks as if the whole solid earth had changed into ice, and broken up!" I said to her, laughing, "I don't wonder that it does, to your inexperienced eyes, my dear." But I had never seen a twentieth part of the quantity, and, in reality, I was pretty much of her opinion.

However, at two p.m. on the afternoon of the sixth day, that is to say, when we were sixty-six days out, John Steadiman who had gone aloft, sang out from the top, that the sea was clear ahead. Before four p.m. a strong breeze springing up right astern, we were in open water at sunset. The breeze then freshening into half a gale of wind, and the Golden Mary being a very fast sailer, we went before the wind merrily, all night.

I had thought it impossible that it could be darker than it had been, until the sun, moon, and stars should fall out of the Heavens, and Time should be destroyed; but, it had been next to light, in comparison with what it was now. The darkness was so profound, that looking into it was painful and oppressive—like looking, without a ray of light, into a dense black bandage put as close before the eyes as it could be, without touching them. I doubled the look-out, and John and I stood in the bow side-by-side, never leaving it all night. Yet I should no more have known that he was near me when he was silent, without putting out my arm and touching him, than I should if he had turned in and been fast asleep below. We were not so much looking out, all of us, as listening to the utmost, both with our eyes and ears.

Next day, I found that the mercury in the barometer, which had risen steadily since we cleared the ice, remained steady. I had had very good observations, with now and then the interruption of a day or so, since our departure. I got the sun at noon, and found that we were in Lat. 58 degrees S., Long. 60 degrees W., off New South Shetland; in the neighbourhood of Cape Horn. We were sixty-seven days out, that day. The ship's reckoning was accurately worked and made up. The ship did her duty admirably, all on board were well, and all hands were as smart, efficient, and contented, as it was possible to be.

When the night came on again as dark as before, it was the eighth night I had been on deck. Nor had I taken more than a very little sleep in the daytime, my station being always near the helm, and often at it, while we were among the ice. Few but those who have tried it can imagine the difficulty and pain of only keeping the eyes open—physically open—under such circumstances, in such darkness. They get struck by the darkness, and blinded by the darkness. They make patterns in it, and they flash in it, as if they had gone out of your head to look at you. On the turn of midnight, John Steadiman, who was alert and fresh (for I had always made him turn in by day), said to me, "Captain Ravender, I entreat of you to go below. I am sure you can hardly stand, and your voice is getting weak, sir. Go below, and take a little rest. I'll call you if a block chafes." I said to John in answer, "Well, well, John! Let us wait till the turn of one o'clock, before we talk about that." I had just had one of the ship's lanterns held up, that I might see how the night went by my watch, and it was then twenty minutes after twelve.

At five minutes before one, John sang out to the boy to bring the lantern again, and when I told him once more what the time was, entreated and prayed of me to go below. "Captain Ravender," says he, "all's well; we can't afford to have you laid up for a single hour; and I respectfully and earnestly beg of you to go below." The end of it was, that I agreed to do so, on the understanding that if I failed to come up of my own accord within three hours, I was to be punctually called. Having settled that, I left John in charge. But I called him to me once afterwards, to ask him a question. I had been to look at the barometer, and had seen the mercury still perfectly steady, and had come up the companion again to take a last look about me—if I can use such a word in reference to such darkness—when I thought that the waves, as the *Golden Mary* parted them and shook them off, had a hollow sound in them; something that I fancied was a rather unusual reverberation. I was standing by the quarter-deck rail on the starboard side, when I called John aft to me, and bade him listen. He did so with the greatest attention. Turning to me he then said, "Rely upon it, Captain Ravender, you have been without rest too long, and the novelty is only in the state of your sense of hearing." I thought so too by that time, and I think so now, though I can never know for absolute certain in this world, whether it was or not.

When I left John Steadiman in charge, the ship was still going at a great rate through the water. The wind still blew right astern. Though she was making great way, she was under shortened sail, and had no more than she could easily carry. All was snug, and nothing complained. There was a pretty sea running, but not a very high sea neither, nor at all a confused one.

I turned in, as we seamen say, all standing. The meaning of that is, I did not pull my clothes off—no, not even so much as my coat: though I did my shoes, for my feet were badly swelled with the deck. There was a little swing-lamp alight in my cabin. I thought, as I looked at it before shutting my eyes, that I was so tired of darkness, and troubled by darkness, that I could have gone to sleep best in the midst of a million of flaming gas-lights. That was the last thought I had before I went off, except the prevailing thought that I should not be able to get to sleep at all.

I dreamed that I was back at Penrith again, and was trying to get round the church, which had altered its shape very much since I last saw it, and was cloven all down the middle of the steeple in a most singular manner. Why I wanted to get round the church I don't know; but I was as anxious to do it as if my life depended on it. Indeed, I believe it did in the dream. For all that, I could not get round the church. I was still trying, when I came against it with a violent shock, and was flung out of my cot against the ship's side. Shrieks and a terrific outcry struck me far harder than the bruising timbers, and amidst sounds of grinding and crashing, and a heavy rushing and breaking of water—sounds I understood too well—I made my way on deck. It was not an easy thing to do, for the ship heeled over frightfully, and was beating in a furious manner.

I could not see the men as I went forward, but I could hear that they were hauling in sail, in disorder. I had my trumpet in my hand, and, after directing and encouraging them in this till it was done, I hailed first John Steadiman, and then my second mate, Mr. William Rames. Both answered clearly and steadily. Now, I had practised them and all my crew, as I have ever made it a custom to practise all who sail with me, to take certain stations and wait my orders, in case of any unexpected crisis. When my voice was heard hailing, and their voices were heard answering, I was aware, through all the noises of the ship and sea, and all the crying of the passengers below, that there was a pause. "Are you ready, Rames?"—"Ay, ay, sir!"—"Then light up, for God's sake!" In a moment he and another were burning blue-lights, and the ship and all on board seemed to be enclosed in a mist of light, under a great black dome.

The light shone up so high that I could see the huge iceberg upon which we had struck, cloven at the top and down the middle, exactly like Penrith

Church in my dream. At the same moment I could see the watch last relieved, crowding up and down on deck; I could see Mrs. Atherfield and Miss Cole-shaw thrown about on the top of the companion as they struggled to bring the child up from below; I could see that the masts were going with the shock and the beating of the ship; I could see the frightful breach stove in on the starboard side, half the length of the vessel, and the sheathing and timbers spirting up; I could see that the Cutter was disabled, in a wreck of broken fragments; and I could see every eye turned upon me. It is my belief that if there had been ten thousand eyes there, I should have seen them all, with their different looks. And all this in a moment. But you must consider what a moment.

I saw the men, as they looked at me, fall towards their appointed stations, like good men and true. If she had not righted, they could have done very little there or anywhere but die—not that it is little for a man to die at his post—I mean they could have done nothing to save the passengers and themselves. Hap-pily, however, the violence of the shock with which we had so determinedly borne down direct on that fatal iceberg, as if it had been our destination instead of our destruction, had so smashed and pounded the ship that she got off in this same instant and righted. I did not want the carpenter to tell me she was fill-ing and going down; I could see and hear that. I gave

Rames the word to lower the Long-boat and the Surf-boat, and I myself told off the men for each duty. Not one hung back, or came before the other. I now whispered to John Steadiman, "John, I stand at the gangway here, to see every soul on board safe over the side. You shall have the next post of honour, and shall be the last but one to leave the ship. Bring up the passengers, and range them behind me; and put what provision and water you can got at, in the boats. Cast your eye for'ard, John, and you'll see you have not a moment to lose."

My noble fellows got the boats over the side as orderly as I ever saw boats lowered with any sea running, and, when they were launched, two or three of the nearest men in them as they held on, rising and falling with the swell, called out, looking up at me, "Captain Ravender, if anything goes wrong with us, and you are saved, remember we stood by you!"— "We'll all stand by one another ashore, yet, please God, my lads!" says I. "Hold on bravely, and be tender with the women."

The women were an example to us. They trembled very much, but they were quiet and perfectly collected. "Kiss me, Captain Ravender," says Mrs. Atherfield, "and God in heaven bless you, you good man!" "My dear," says I, "those words are better for me than a life-boat." I held her child in my arms till she was in the boat, and then kissed the child and handed her safe down. I now said to the people in her, "You have got your freight, my lads, all but me, and I am not coming yet awhile. Pull away from the ship, and keep off!"

That was the Long-boat. Old Mr. Rarx was one of her complement, and he was the only passenger who had greatly misbehaved since the ship struck. Others had been a little wild, which was not to be wondered at, and not very blamable; but, he had made a lamentation and uproar which it was danger-ous for the people to hear, as there is always conta-gion in weakness and selfishness. His incessant cry had been that he must not be separated from the child, that he couldn't see the child, and that he and the child must go together. He had even tried to wrest the child out of my arms, that he might keep her in his. "Mr. Rarx," said I to him when it came to that, "I have a loaded pistol in my pocket; and if you don't stand out of the gangway, and keep perfectly quiet, I shall shoot you through the heart, if you have got one." Says he, "You won't do murder, Captain Raven-der!" "No, sir," says I, "I won't murder forty-four people to humour you, but I'll shoot you to save them." After that he was quiet, and stood shivering a little way off, until I named him to go over the side.

The Long-boat being cast off, the Surf-boat was soon filled. There only remained aboard the *Golden Mary*, John Mullion the man who had kept on burning the blue-lights (and who had lighted every new one at every old one before it went out, as quietly as if he had been at an illumination); John Steadiman; and myself. I hurried those two into the Surf-boat, called to them to keep off, and waited with a grateful and relieved heart for the Long-boat to come and take me in, if she could. I looked at my watch, and it showed me, by the blue-light, ten minutes past two. They lost no time. As soon as she was near enough, I swung myself into her, and called to the men, "With a will, lads! She's reeling!" We were not an inch too far out of the inner vortex of her going down, when, by the blue-light which John Mullion still burnt in the bow of the Surf-boat, we saw her lurch, and plunge to the bottom head-foremost. The child cried, weeping wildly, "O the dear *Golden Mary*! O look at her! Save her! Save the poor *Golden Mary*!" And then the light burnt out, and the black dome seemed to come down upon us.

I suppose if we had all stood a-top of a mountain, and seen the whole remainder of the world sink away from under us, we could hardly have felt more shocked and solitary than we did when we knew we were alone on the wide ocean, and that the beautiful ship in which most of us had been securely asleep within half an hour was gone for ever. There was an awful silence in our boat, and such a kind of palsy on the rowers and the man at the rudder, that I felt they were scarcely keeping her before the sea. I spoke out then, and said, "Let every one here thank the Lord for our preservation!" All the voices answered (even the child's), "We thank the Lord!" I then said the Lord's Prayer, and all hands said it after me with a solemn murmuring. Then I gave the word "Cheerily, O men, Cheerily!" and I felt that they were handling the boat again as a boat ought to be handled.

The Surf-boat now burnt another blue-light to show us where they were, and we made for her, and laid ourselves as nearly alongside of her as we dared. I had always kept my boats with a coil or two of good stout stuff in each of them, so both boats had a rope at hand. We made a shift, with much labour and trouble, to got near enough to one another to divide the blue-lights (they were no use after that night, for the sea-water soon got at them), and to get a tow-rope out between us. All night long we kept together, sometimes obliged to cast off the rope, and some-times getting it out again, and all of us wearying for the morning—which appeared so long in coming that old Mr. Rarx screamed out, in spite of his fears of me, "The world is drawing to an end, and the sun will never rise any more!"

When the day broke, I found that we were all huddled together in a miserable manner. We were deep in the water; being, as I found on mustering, thirty-one in number, or at least six too many. In the Surf-boat they were fourteen in number, being at least four too many. The first thing I did, was to get myself passed to the rudder—which I took from that time—and to get Mrs. Atherfield, her child, and Miss Coleshaw, passed on to sit next me. As to old Mr. Rarx, I put him in the bow, as far from us as I could. And I put some of the best men near us in order that if I should drop there might be a skillful hand ready to take the helm.

The sea moderating as the sun came up, though the sky was cloudy and wild, we spoke the other boat, to know what stores they had, and to overhaul what we had. I had a compass in my pocket, a small telescope, a double-barrelled pistol, a knife, and a fire-box and matches. Most of my men had knives, and some had a little tobacco: some, a pipe as well. We had a mug among us, and an iron spoon. As to provisions, there were in my boat two bags of biscuit, one piece of raw beef, one piece of raw pork, a bag of coffee, roasted but not ground (thrown in, I imagine, by mistake, for something else), two small casks of water, and about half-a-gallon of rum in a keg. The Surf-boat, having rather more rum than we, and fewer to drink it, gave us, as I estimated, another quart into our keg. In return, we gave them three double handfuls of coffee, tied up in a piece of a handkerchief; they reported that they had aboard besides, a bag of biscuit, a piece of beef, a small cask of water, a small box of lemons, and a Dutch cheese. It took a long time to make these exchanges, and they were not made without risk to both parties; the sea running quite high enough to make our approaching near to one another very hazardous. In the bundle with the coffee, I conveyed to John Steadiman (who had a ship's compass with him), a paper written in pencil, and torn from my pocket-book, containing the course I meant to steer, in the hope of making land, or being picked up by some vessel—I say in the hope, though I had little hope of either deliverance. I then sang out to him, so as all might hear, that if we two boats could live or die together, we would; but, that if we should be parted by the weather, and join company no more, they should have our prayers and blessings, and we asked for theirs. We then gave them three cheers, which they returned, and I saw the men's heads droop in both boats as they fell to their oars again.

These arrangements had occupied the general attention advantageously for all, though (as I expressed in the last sentence) they ended in a sorrowful feeling. I now said a few words to my fellow-voyagers on the subject of the small stock of food on which our lives depended if they were preserved from the great deep, and on the rigid necessity of our eking it out in the most frugal manner. One and all replied that whatever allowance I thought best to lay down should be strictly kept to. We made a pair of scales out of a thin scrap of iron-plating and some twine, and I got together for weights such of the heaviest buttons among us as I calculated made up some fraction over two ounces. This was the allowance of solid food served out once a-day to each, from that time to the end; with the addition of a coffee-berry, or sometimes half a one, when the weather was very fair, for breakfast. We had nothing else whatever, but half a pint of water each per day, and sometimes, when we were coldest and weakest, a teaspoonful of rum each, served out as a dram. I know how learnedly it can be shown that rum is poison, but I also know that in this case, as in all similar cases I have ever read of—which are numerous—no words can express the comfort and support derived from it. Nor have I the least doubt that it saved the lives of far more than half our number. Having mentioned half a pint of water as our daily allowance, I ought to observe that sometimes we had less, and sometimes we had more; for much rain fell, and we caught it in a canvas stretched for the purpose.

Thus, at that tempestuous time of the year, and in that tempestuous part of the world, we shipwrecked people rose and fell with the waves. It is not my intention to relate (if I can avoid it) such circumstances appertaining to our doleful condition as have been better told in many other narratives of the kind than

I can be expected to tell them. I will only note, in so many passing words, that day after day and night after night, we received the sea upon our backs to prevent it from swamping the boat; that one party was always kept baling, and that every hat and cap among us soon got worn out, though patched up fifty times, as the only vessels we had for that service; that another party lay down in the bottom of the boat, while a third rowed; and that we were soon all in boils and blisters and rags.

The other boat was a source of such anxious interest to all of us that I used to wonder whether, if we were saved, the time could ever come when the survivors in this boat of ours could be at all indifferent to the fortunes of the survivors in that. We got out a tow-rope whenever the weather permitted, but that did not often happen, and how we two parties kept within the same horizon, as we did, He, who mercifully permitted it to be so for our consolation, only knows. I never shall forget the looks with which, when the morning light came, we used to gaze about us over the stormy waters, for the other boat. We once parted company for seventy-two hours, and we believed them to have gone down, as they did us. The joy on both sides when we came within view of one another again, had something in a manner Divine in it; each was so forgetful of individual suffering, in tears of delight and sympathy for the people in the other boat.

I have been wanting to get round to the individual or personal part of my subject, as I call it, and the foregoing incident puts me in the right way. The patience and good disposition aboard of us, was wonderful. I was not surprised by it in the women; for all men born of women know what great qualities they will show when men will fail; but, I own I was a little surprised by it in some of the men. Among one-and-thirty people assembled at the best of times, there will usually, I should say, be two or three uncertain tempers. I knew that I had more than one rough temper with me among my own people, for I had chosen those for the Long-boat that I might have them under my eye. But, they softened under their misery, and were as considerate of the ladies, and as compassionate of the child, as the best among us, or among men—they could not have been more so. I heard scarcely any complaining. The party lying down would moan a good deal in their sleep, and I would often notice a man—not always the same man, it is to be understood, but nearly all of them at one time or other—sitting moaning at his oar, or in his place, as he looked mistily over the sea. When it happened to be long before I could catch his eye, he would go on moaning all the time in the dismallest manner; but, when our looks met, he would brighten and leave off. I almost always got the impression that he did not know what sound he had been making, but that he thought he had been humming a tune.

Our sufferings from cold and wet were far greater than our sufferings from hunger. We managed to keep the child warm; but, I doubt if any one else among us ever was warm for five minutes together; and the shivering, and the chattering of teeth, were sad to hear. The child cried a little at first for her lost playfellow, the *Golden Mary*; but hardly ever whimpered afterwards; and when the state of the weather made it possible, she used now and then to be held up in the arms of some of us, to look over the sea for John Steadiman's boat. I see the golden hair and the innocent face now, between me and the driving clouds, like an angel going to fly away.

It had happened on the second day, towards night, that Mrs. Atherfield, in getting Little Lucy to sleep, sang her a song. She had a soft, melodious voice, and, when she had finished it, our people up and begged for another. She sang them another, and after it had fallen dark ended with the Evening Hymn. From that time, whenever anything could be heard above the sea and wind, and while she had any voice left, nothing would serve the people but that she should sing at sunset. She always did, and always ended with the Evening Hymn. We mostly took up the last line, and shed tears when it was done, but not miserably.

We had a prayer night and morning, also, when the weather allowed of it.

Twelve nights and eleven days we had been driving in the boat, when old Mr. Rarx began to be delirious, and to cry out to me to throw the gold overboard or it would sink us, and we should all be lost. For days past the child had been declining, and that was the great cause of his wildness. He had been over and over again shrieking out to me to give her all the remaining meat, to give her all the remaining rum, to save her at any cost, or we should all be ruined. At this time, she lay in her mother's arms at my feet. One of her little hands was almost always creeping about her mother's neck or chin. I had watched the wasting of the little hand, and I knew it was nearly over.

The old man's cries were so discordant with the mother's love and submission, that I called out to him in an angry voice, unless he held his peace on the instant, I would order him to be knocked on the head and thrown overboard. He was mute then, until the child died, very peacefully, an hour afterwards: which was known to all in the boat by the mother's breaking out into lamentations for the first time since the wreck—for, she had great fortitude and constancy, though she was a little gentle woman. Old Mr. Rarx then became quite ungovernable, tearing what rags he had on him, raging in imprecations, and calling to me that if I had thrown the gold over-board (always the gold with him!) I might have saved the child. "And now," says he, in a terrible voice, "we shall founder, and all go to the Devil, for our sins will sink us, when we have no innocent child to bear us up!" We so discovered with amaze-ment, that this old wretch had only cared for the life of the pretty little creature dear to all of us, because of the influence he superstitiously hoped she might have in preserving him! Altogether it was too much for the smith or armourer, who was sitting next the old man, to bear. He took him by the throat and rolled him under the thwarts, where he lay still enough for hours afterwards.

All that thirteenth night, Miss Coleshaw, lying across my knees as I kept the helm, comforted and supported the poor mother. Her child, covered with a pea-jacket of mine, lay in her lap. It troubled me all night to think that there was no Prayer-Book among us, and that I could remember but very few of the exact words of the burial service. When I stood up at broad day, all knew what was going to be done, and I noticed that my poor fellows made the motion of uncovering their heads, though their heads had been stark bare to the sky and sea for many a weary hour. There was a long heavy swell on, but otherwise it was a fair morning, and there were broad fields of sunlight on the waves in the east. I said no more than this: "I am the Resurrection and the Life, saith the Lord. He raised the daughter of Jairus the ruler, and said she was not dead but slept. He raised the widow's son. He arose Himself, and was seen of many. He loved little children, saying, Suffer them to come unto Me and rebuke them not, for of such is the kingdom of heaven. In His name, my friends, and committed to His merciful goodness!" With those words I laid my rough face softly on the placid little forehead, and buried the Golden Lucy in the grave of the *Golden Mary*.

Having had it on my mind to relate the end of this dear little child, I have omitted something from its exact place, which I will supply here. It will come quite as well here as anywhere else.

Foreseeing that if the boat lived through the stormy weather, the time must come, and soon come, when we should have absolutely no morsel to eat, I had one momentous point often in my thoughts. Although I had, years before that, fully satisfied myself that the instances in which human beings in the last distress have fed upon each other, are exceedingly few, and have very seldom indeed (if ever) occurred when the people in distress, however dreadful their extremity, have been accustomed to moderate forbearance and restraint; I say, though I had long before quite satisfied my mind on this topic, I felt doubtful whether there might not have been in former cases some harm and danger from keeping it out of sight and pretending not to think of it. I felt doubtful whether some minds, growing weak with fasting and exposure and having such a terrific idea to dwell upon in secret, might not magnify it until it got to have an awful attraction about it. This was not a new thought of mine, for it had grown out of my reading. However, it came over me stronger than it had ever done before—as it had reason for doing—in the boat, and on the fourth day I decided that I would bring out into the light that unformed fear which must have been more or less darkly in every brain among us. Therefore, as a means of beguiling the time and inspiring hope, I gave them the best summary in my power of Bligh's voyage of more than three thousand miles, in an open boat, after the Mutiny of the *Bounty*, and of the wonderful preservation of that boat's crew. They listened throughout with great interest, and I concluded by telling them, that, in my opinion, the happiest circumstance in the whole narrative was, that Bligh, who was no delicate man either, had solemnly placed it on record therein that he was sure and certain that under no conceivable circumstances whatever would that emaciated party, who had gone through all the pains of famine, have preyed on one another. I cannot describe the visible relief which this spread through the boat, and how the tears stood in every eye. From that time I was as well convinced as Bligh himself that there was no danger, and that this phantom, at any rate, did not haunt us.

Now, it was a part of Bligh's experience that when the people in his boat were most cast down, nothing did them so much good as hearing a story told by one of their number. When I mentioned that, I saw that it struck the general attention as much as it did my own, for I had not thought of it until I came to it in my summary. This was on the day after Mrs. Atherfield first sang to us. I proposed that, whenever the weather would permit, we should have a story two hours after dinner (I always issued the allowance I have mentioned at one o'clock, and called it by that name), as well as our song at sunset. The proposal was received with a cheerful satisfaction that warmed my heart within me; and I do not say too much when I say that those two periods in the four-and-twenty hours were expected with positive pleasure, and were really enjoyed by all hands. Spectres as we soon were in our bodily wasting, our imaginations did not perish like the gross flesh upon our bones. Music and Adventure, two of the great gifts of Providence to mankind, could charm us long after that was lost.

The wind was almost always against us after the second day; and for many days together we could not nearly hold our own. We had all varieties of bad weather. We had rain, hail, snow, wind, mist, thunder and lightning. Still the boats lived through the heavy seas, and still we perishing people rose and fell with the great waves.

Sixteen nights and fifteen days, twenty nights and nineteen days, twenty-four nights and twenty-three days. So the time went on. Disheartening as I knew that our progress, or want of progress, must be, I never deceived them as to my calculations of it. In the first place, I felt that we were all too near eternity for deceit; in the second place, I knew that if I failed, or died, the man who followed me must have a knowledge of the true state of things to begin upon. When I told them at noon, what I reckoned we had made or lost, they generally received what I said in a tranquil and resigned manner, and always gratefully towards me. It was not unusual at any time of the day for some one to burst out weeping loudly without any new cause; and, when the burst was over, to calm down a little better than before. I had seen exactly the same thing in a house of mourning.

During the whole of this time, old Mr. Rarx had had his fits of calling out to me to throw the gold (always the gold!) overboard, and of heaping violent reproaches upon me for not having saved the child; but now, the food being all gone, and I having noth-ing left to serve out but a bit of coffee-berry now and then, he began to be too weak to do this, and consequently fell silent. Mrs. Atherfield and Miss

Coleshaw generally lay, each with an arm across one
of my knees, and her head upon it. They never complained at all. Up to the time of her child's death,
Mrs. Atherfield had bound up her own beautiful
hair every day; and I took particular notice that this
was always before she sang her song at night, when
everyone looked at her. But she never did it after the
loss of her darling; and it would have been now all
tangled with dirt and wet, but that Miss Coleshaw
was careful of it long after she was herself, and
would sometimes smooth it down with her weak
thin hands.

We were past mustering a story now; but one day,
at about this period, I reverted to the superstition of
old Mr. Rarx, concerning the Golden Lucy, and told
them that nothing vanished from the eye of God,
though much might pass away from the eyes of men.
"We were all of us," says I, "children once; and our
baby feet have strolled in green woods ashore; and
our baby hands have gathered flowers in gardens,
where the birds were singing. The children that we
were, are not lost to the great knowledge of our
Creator. Those innocent creatures will appear with
us before Him, and plead for us. What we were in
the best time of our generous youth will arise and go
with us too. The purest part of our lives will not
desert us at the pass to which all of us here present
are gliding. What we were then, will be as much in

existence before Him, as what we are now." They were no less comforted by this consideration, than I was myself; and Miss Coleshaw, drawing my ear nearer to her lips, said, "Captain Ravender, I was on my way to marry a disgraced and broken man, whom I dearly loved when he was honourable and good. Your words seem to have come out of my own poor heart." She pressed my hand upon it, smiling.

Twenty-seven nights and twenty-six days. We were in no want of rain-water, but we had nothing else. And yet, even now, I never turned my eyes upon a waking face but it tried to brighten before mine. O, what a thing it is, in a time of danger and in the presence of death, the shining of a face upon a face! I have heard it broached that orders should be given in great new ships by electric telegraph. I admire machinery as much as any man, and am as thankful to it as any man can be for what it does for us. But it will never be a substitute for the face of a man, with his soul in it, encouraging another man to be brave and true. Never try it for that. It will break down like a straw.

I now began to remark certain changes in myself which I did not like. They caused me much disquiet. I often saw the Golden Lucy in the air above the boat. I often saw her I have spoken of before, sitting beside me. I saw the *Golden Mary* go down, as she really had gone down, twenty times in a day. And yet the sea was mostly, to my thinking, not sea neither, but moving country and extraordinary mountainous regions, the like of which have never been beheld. I felt it time to leave my last words regarding John Steadiman, in case any lips should last out to repeat them to any living ears. I said that John had told me (as he had on deck) that he had sung out "Breakers ahead!" the instant they were audible, and had tried to wear ship, but she struck before it could be done. (His cry, I dare say, had made my dream.) I said that the circumstances were altogether without warning, and out of any course that could have been guarded against; that the same loss would have happened if I had been in charge; and that John was not to blame, but from first to last had done his duty nobly, like the man he was. I tried to write it down in my pocket-book, but could make no words, though I knew what the words were that I wanted to make. When it had come to that, her hands— though she was dead so long—laid me down gently in the bottom of the boat, and she and the Golden Lucy swung me to sleep.

★ ★ ★ ★ ★

All that follows, was written by John Steadiman, Chief Mate:

On the twenty-sixth day after the foundering of the *Golden Mary* at sea, I, John Steadiman, was sitting in my place in the stern-sheets of the Surf-boat, with just sense enough left in me to steer—that is to say, with my eyes strained, wide-awake, over the bows of the boat, and my brains fast asleep and dreaming— when I was roused upon a sudden by our second mate, Mr. William Rames.

"Let me take a spell in your place," says he. "And look you out for the Long-boat astern. The last time she rose on the crest of a wave, I thought I made out a signal flying aboard her."

We shifted our places, clumsily and slowly enough, for we were both of us weak and dazed with wet, cold, and hunger. I waited some time, watching the heavy rollers astern, before the Long-boat rose a-top of one of them at the same time with us. At last, she was heaved up for a moment well in view, and there, sure enough, was the signal flying aboard of her—a strip of rag of some sort, rigged to an oar, and hoisted in her bows.

"What does it mean?" says Rames to me in a qua-vering, trembling sort of voice. "Do they signal a sail in sight?"

"Hush, for God's sake!" says I, clapping my hand over his mouth. "Don't let the people hear you. They'll all go mad together if we mislead them about that signal. Wait a bit, till I have another look at it."

I held on by him, for he had set me all of a tremble with his notion of a sail in sight, and watched for the

Long-boat again. Up she rose on the top of another roller. I made out the signal clearly, that second time, and saw that it was rigged half-mast high.

"Rames," says I, "it's a signal of distress. Pass the word forward to keep her before the sea, and no more. We must get the Long-boat within hailing distance of us, as soon as possible."

I dropped down into my old place at the tiller without another word—for the thought went through me like a knife that something had happened to Captain Ravender. I should consider myself unworthy to write another line of this statement, if I had not made up my mind to speak the truth, the whole truth, and nothing but the truth—and I must, therefore, confess plainly that now, for the first time, my heart sank within me. This weakness on my part was produced in some degree, as I take it, by the exhausting effects of previous anxiety and grief.

Our provisions—if I may give that name to what we had left—were reduced to the rind of one lemon and about a couple of handsfull of coffee-berries. Besides these great distresses, caused by the death, the danger, and the suffering among my crew and passengers, I had had a little distress of my own to shake me still more, in the death of the child whom I had got to be very fond of on the voyage out—so fond that I was secretly a little jealous of her being taken in the Long-boat instead of mine when the ship foundered. It used to be a great comfort to me, and I think to those with me also, after we had seen the last of the *Golden Mary*, to see the Golden Lucy, held up by the men in the Long-boat, when the weather allowed it, as the best and brightest sight they had to show. She looked, at the distance we saw her from, almost like a little white bird in the air. To miss her for the first time, when the weather lulled a little again, and we all looked out for our white bird and looked in vain, was a sore disappointment. To see the men's heads bowed down and the captain's hand pointing into the sea when we hailed the Long-boat, a few days after, gave me as heavy a shock and as sharp a pang of heartache to bear as ever I remember suffering in all my life. I only mention these things to show that if I did give way a little at first, under the dread that our captain was lost to us, it was not without having been a good deal shaken beforehand by more trials of one sort or another than often fall to one man's share.

I had got over the choking in my throat with the help of a drop of water, and had steadied my mind again so as to be prepared against the worst, when I heard the hail (Lord help the poor fellows, how weak it sounded!)—

"Surf-boat, ahoy!"

I looked up, and there were our companions in misfortune tossing abreast of us; not so near that we could make out the features of any of them, but near enough, with some exertion for people in our condition, to make their voices heard in the intervals when the wind was weakest.

I answered the hail, and waited a bit, and heard nothing, and then sung out the captain's name. The voice that replied did not sound like his; the words that reached us were:

"Chief-mate wanted on board!"

Every man of my crew knew what that meant as well as I did. As second officer in command, there could be but one reason for wanting me on board the Long-boat. A groan went all round us, and my men looked darkly in each other's faces, and whispered under their breaths:

"The captain is dead!"

I commanded them to be silent, and not to make too sure of bad news, at such a pass as things had now come to with us. Then, hailing the Long-boat, I signified that I was ready to go on board when the weather would let me—stopped a bit to draw a good long breath—and then called out as loud as I could the dreadful question:

"Is the captain dead?"

The black figures of three or four men in the after-part of the Long-boat all stooped down together as my voice reached them. They were lost to view for about a minute; then appeared again—one man among them was held up on his feet by the rest, and he hailed back the blessed words (a very faint hope went a very long way with people in our desperate situation): "Not yet!"

The relief felt by me, and by all with me, when we knew that our captain, though unfitted for duty, was not lost to us, it is not in words—at least, not in such words as a man like me can command—to express. I did my best to cheer the men by telling them what a good sign it was that we were not as badly off yet as we had feared; and then communicated what instructions I had to give, to William Rames, who was to be left in command in my place when I took charge of the Long-boat. After that, there was nothing to be done, but to wait for the chance of the wind dropping at sunset, and the sea going down afterwards, so as to enable our weak crews to lay the two boats alongside of each other, without undue risk—or, to put it plainer, without saddling ourselves with the necessity for any extraordinary exertion of strength or skill. Both the one and the other had now been starved out of us for days and days together.

At sunset the wind suddenly dropped, but the sea, which had been running high for so long a time past, took hours after that before it showed any signs of getting to rest. The moon was shining, the sky was wonderfully clear, and it could not have been, according to my calculations, far off midnight, when the long, slow, regular swell of the calming ocean fairly set in, and I took the responsibility of lessening the distance between the Long-boat and ourselves.

It was, I dare say, a delusion of mine; but I thought I had never seen the moon shine so white and ghastly anywhere, either on sea or on land, as she shone that night while we were approaching our companions in misery. When there was not much more than a boat's length between us, and the white light streamed cold and clear over all our faces, both crews rested on their oars with one great shudder, and stared over the gunwale of either boat, panic-stricken at the first sight of each other.

"Any lives lost among you?" I asked, in the midst of that frightful silence.

The men in the Long-bout huddled together like sheep at the sound of my voice.

"None yet, but the child, thanks be to God!" answered one among them.

And at the sound of his voice, all my men shrank together like the men in the Long-boat. I was afraid to let the horror produced by our first meeting at close quarters after the dreadful changes that wet, cold, and famine had produced, last one moment longer than could be helped; so, without giving time for any more questions and answers, I commanded the men to lay the two boats close alongside of each other. When I rose up and committed the tiller to the hands of Rames, all my poor follows raised their white faces imploringly to mine. "Don't leave us, sir," they said, "don't leave us." "I leave you," says I, "under the command and the guidance of Mr. William Rames, as good a sailor as I am, and as trusty and kind a man as ever stepped. Do your duty by him, as you have done it by me; and remember to the last, that while there is life there is hope. God bless and help you all!" With those words I collected what strength I had left, and caught at two arms that were held out to me, and so got from the stern-sheets of one boat into the stern-sheets of the other.

"Mind where you step, sir," whispered one of the men who had helped me into the Long-boat. I looked down as he spoke. Three figures were huddled up below me, with the moonshine falling on them in ragged streaks through the gaps between the men standing or sitting above them. The first face I made out was the face of Miss Coleshaw, her eyes were wide open and fixed on me. She seemed still to keep her senses, and, by the alternate parting and closing of her lips, to be trying to speak, but I could not hear that she uttered a single word. On her shoulder rested the head of Mrs. Atherfield. The mother of our poor little Golden Lucy must, I think, have been dreaming of the child she had lost; for there was a faint smile just ruffling the white stillness of her face, when I first saw it turned upward, with peaceful closed eyes towards the heavens. From her, I looked down a little, and there, with his head on her lap, and with one of her hands resting tenderly on his cheek—there lay the Captain, to whose help and guidance, up to this miserable time, we had never looked in vain,—there, worn out at last in our service, and for our sakes, lay the best and bravest man of all our company. I stole my hand in gently through his clothes and laid it on his heart, and felt a little feeble warmth over it, though my cold dulled touch could not detect even the faintest beating. The two men in the stern-sheets with me, noticing what I was doing—knowing I loved him like a brother—and seeing, I suppose, more distress in my face than I my-self was conscious of its showing, lost command over themselves altogether, and burst into a piteous moan-ing, sobbing lamentation over him. One of the two drew aside a jacket from his feet, and showed me that they were bare, except where a wet, ragged strip of stocking still clung to one of them. When the ship struck the iceberg, he had run on deck leaving his shoes in his cabin. All through the voyage in the boat his feet had been unprotected; and not a soul had dis-covered it until he dropped! As long as he could keep his eyes open, the very look of them had cheered the men, and comforted and upheld the women. Not one living creature in the boat, with any sense about him, but had felt the good influence of that brave man in one way or another. Not one but had heard him, over and over again, give the credit to others which was due only to himself; praising this man for patience, and thanking that man for help, when the patience and the help had really and truly, as to the best part of both, come only from him. All this, and much more, I heard pouring confusedly from the men's lips while they crouched down, sobbing and crying over their commander, and wrapping the jacket as warmly and tenderly as they could over his cold feet. It went to my heart to check them; but I knew that if this lamenting spirit spread any further, all chance of keeping alight any last sparks of hope and resolution among the boat's company would be lost for ever. Accordingly I sent them to their places, spoke a few encouraging words to the men forward, promising to serve out, when the morning came, as much as I dared, of any eatable thing left in the lockers; called to Rames, in my old boat, to keep as near us as he safely could; drew the garments and coverings of the two poor suffering women more closely about them; and, with a secret prayer to be directed for the best in bearing the awful responsibility now laid on my shoulders, took my Captain's vacant place at the helm of the Long-boat.

This, as well as I can tell it, is the full and true account of how I came to be placed in charge of the lost passengers and crew of the *Golden Mary*, on the morning of the twenty-seventh day after the ship struck the iceberg, and foundered at sea.